Raising Miss Lili

A novella by Jim Hamilton

This is a work of fiction. Names, characters, businesses, places, events, locales, and incidents are either the products of the author's imagination or used in a fictitious manner. Any resemblance to actual persons, living or dead, or actual events, is purely coincidental.

(C) Copyright 2019 by Jim Hamilton

ISBN: *9781794534575*

*Dedicated to my wife, Linda,
and my three wonderful children:
Nelson, James, and Sarah.*

*Cover artwork
and frontispiece
by the author.*

Also by Jim Hamilton:

The Chaos Machine*
The da Vinci Butterfly
Second Contact*
Mankind 2.0*
Colony Ship New Hope
Goddess of the Gillani
The Race at Valli Ha'i

* Combined in *The Chaos Trilogy*
"A trilogy of exuberant and lucid tales ..." — *Kirkus Reviews.*

Table of Contents

Prologue..5
Chapter One..7
Chapter Two..31
Chapter Three..33
Chapter Four..41
Chapter Five..79
Chapter Six..93
Chapter Seven...95
Chapter Eight..121
Chapter Nine...123
Chapter Ten...143
Chapter Eleven..145
Author's Note..167

Raising Miss Ellie

Prologue

The young boy looked up as the old woman entered the room. He was sitting in an upholstered chair that he had positioned so that he could sit and look out the window. A frown crossed his face as he turned to address his intruder, "Whatever you want, I'm not in the mood today, so go away." He turned back to gaze out of the window again.

The elderly woman smiled, "Is that any way to behave?" She stepped around the chair to face the young lad directly. "You've been neglecting your chores for some time now."

"So what?"

"We all have our place in the grand scheme of things, you know." She shook her head, "My job, unfortunately, is to make sure that you do your part."

He sighed, "Just go away and leave me alone."

The woman paused for a moment before continuing, "If you'll buckle down and take care of my current to-do list, you can go outside for a spell."

The boy perked up a bit, "How long is the list?"

She pulled a card from her tunic and handed it to him, "Not that many. While you've been—umm—on hiatus, the others have taken care of what they could."

He looked at the card and scanned the list. "Okay. Fine." He looked up at her, "And once I finish these, you'll let me out for a while?"

"Yes." She held out her hand, "Is it a deal?"

He grinned and shook her large hand with his small one, "It's a deal."

Chapter One

Right before dawn, Mary Ellen was awakened by the crowing of her two roosters. She lay in her four-poster for a few moments before throwing back the covers and getting out of bed. It was cold in the house and she grabbed her robe off the back of the rocking chair and pulled it on. She could tell by the aches in her joints that there was a rainstorm coming—by early afternoon at the latest. Stepping over to the window, she pulled back the drapes and admired the bright pink colors that were painted on the clouds by the sun, still below the horizon. "Red sky at morning, sailors take warning," she recited out loud. As she made her way down the narrow hallway to the bathroom, the roosters crowed again, each trying to outdo the other. After relieving her nearly full bladder, she stood before the small sink and turned on the tap. She held her hands underneath the running water and scrubbed them thoroughly with soap and then captured some of the water to splash on her face. The chilled liquid was akin to a hearty slap, instantly bringing her wide awake. She grabbed the hand towel and dried her face before picking up her brush and battling her long gray hair into submission. Gathering her tresses at the back of her head, she deftly coiled the gathered hair into a bun and fixed it in place with several hairpins. She stared at herself in the mirror and saw an old lady staring back at her. Her once vivid blue eyes had gone to grey which seemed to complement her hair. Her skin was leathery and wrinkled from a lifetime in the sun with deep creases at the corners of her mouth and eyes. She smiled and her reflection smiled in return. She laughed and it laughed right back at her. "Time to get going," she said to her reflection, which nodded in agreement.

After donning a sweatshirt, overalls, and boots, she headed for the henhouse to gather the eggs. Most of them were in the nesting boxes built for that purpose while the others were scattered around the fenced-in yard, hidden in the tall weeds. She took all that she could find in the yard before entering the dilapidated structure. Taking the eggs from each nest, she left the ones that had her tell-tale X on them—in a week or so, there would be a new brood of chicks running around the place. Carefully setting down her now-full basket, she opened a cupboard and removed the small bag of grain from which she drew handfuls of ground corn and sprinkled them liberally around the yard. Stowing the bag, she closed up the cupboard and returned to the house where she swapped her basket for a milk pail and headed to the barn.

Entering the small structure, she opened the gate to the first stall, "Good morning, Bessie!" The cow watched her with placid eyes, turning its head as Mary Ellen dragged the small stool in place and sat down with the pail between her legs. She hefted the udder, "You're pretty full today, old girl." Grabbing two of the three teats, she began to squeeze and massage them, directing the streams of warm milk into the bucket. After about fifteen minutes, she had filled the bucket about halfway and Bessie's tank had run dry. She patted her on the side of her long nose, "We're done, girl. Time for breakfast." She picked up the pail and left the barn, leaving the doors open so that Bessie could make her way to the field.

While she would normally scramble three of the eggs for breakfast, she decided to drive into town and eat at the diner instead. Placing the basket and pail in the refrigerator, she grabbed her car keys and purse and entered the attached garage through the door in the kitchen. Pushing at the garage door, it rotated upwards, letting in the morning light which illuminated her faded and rusty car. Once a proud coral and white, the Bel Air was a vague color mottled with brownish patches, mostly along the bottom panels. It was the very first car that she had bought for herself and it still ran like a top, even if it looked like a refugee from the scrapyard.

"*Kind of like me*," she thought to herself as she turned the key—smiling as the engine caught right away and purred to life. It was the first Friday of the month and the monthly bills would be due soon. She always liked to pay ahead of time so that there was no chance of being hit with a late fee. She reached the end of her driveway and turned left onto the highway. As she drove along, she glanced at the sky and it confirmed her prediction. A storm was on the way and she wanted to get to town and back before it broke.

* * *

About twenty-five minutes later, she pulled into the parking lot in front of Dinah's Diner, parking near the end of the line of vehicles. Getting out of her car, she noticed that the diner was already half full. She made her way to the door and stepped inside, glancing around. To her relief, her favorite booth was unoccupied and she headed for it where she eased herself onto the padded bench seat.

"Good morning, Miss Ellie!" said a middle-aged woman, as she approached the booth and placed a cup of coffee on the table.

"Good morning to you, too, Gretchen. Although I dare say that we'll see a decent storm sometime after lunch."

Gretchen sighed, "Wouldn't you know it? I just washed my car yesterday." She looked at Mary Ellen, "I assume that you're having your usual?"

"Well, of course." Mary Ellen shook her head, "It's a bit sad to realize that I've become such a creature of habit."

"I don't think that there's anything wrong with that."

"A foolish consistency is the hobgoblin of little minds," replied Mary Ellen.

Gretchen laughed, "What did Emerson know? He died almost 150 years ago." She glanced at the serving window, "I've got an order ready that I need to tend to." She winked, "I'll be back with your hobgoblin as soon as it's ready."

Mary Ellen sipped her coffee as she studied the other customers. She knew most of them and as she made eye contact with each, they smiled or nodded in greeting. However, in the front corner booth was a young couple she didn't recognize. Living in a county with less than 500 people, it was unusual to see newcomers. Probably just passing through, but the highway that ran through the center of town didn't come from anywhere and didn't go anywhere. At least not anywhere important.

Gretchen returned with her order, "One hobgoblin with a side of apple strudel to cure your little mind." She saw the look, "Don't worry, Miss Ellie, the strudel's on the house."

"Why, thank you, Gretchen." She nodded at the strudel, "It's a little out of my comfort zone, but I'll deal with it."

"It's fresh out of the oven—pure heaven," smiled the waitress.

Mary Ellen glanced over at the young couple, "What's the story on booth seven?"

Gretchen looked their way before replying, "Newlyweds from Mobile on their way to Chicago."

Mary Ellen looked surprised, "Aren't they a little off-course?"

"According to the husband, their GPS system told them to go this way. By the time they figured it out, it was quicker to go on than to turn back."

Mary Ellen rolled her eyes, "They used to give out these things that you could fold up and place in the glove box."

"You mean a map?" asked Gretchen. "I never could figure out how to work one of those things."

"Just a glance at one would convince you not to come this way. That's why Eisenhower invented the interstates, you know."

It was Gretchen's turn to roll her eyes, "I'm going to leave you alone for a while to enjoy your usual." She pointed at the apple strudel, "And I'm expecting you to eat that, however unusual the experience might be." She turned and headed for the kitchen.

While she ate her omelet and hash browns, Mary Ellen watched the young couple for a bit, their interaction obvious to her now that she knew more about them. They had wandered hundreds of miles out of the way, but seemed to taking it in stride. Mary Ellen nodded to herself, seeing it as a good sign of the future of their marriage. She polished off the eggs and potatoes and confronted the apple strudel. Dessert had no place at breakfast, in her opinion, but she bravely forked off a bit and placed it in her mouth. As she chewed it slowly, she reflected that maybe this wasn't so bad after all. Taking a sip of milk, she followed it with a much larger piece of strudel. By the time she had scraped the small plate clean, she had decided to make it a permanent addition to her usual. Finishing off her milk and then her coffee, she slid out of the booth and walked to the front where the cash register was located.

Spotting her, Gretchen came over, "I see that you polished off your apple strudel."

"You were right, of course. A little bit of heaven in my life wouldn't hurt."

Gretchen smiled, "I knew you'd like it." She rang up the order, "That'll be $7.67, Miss Ellie. As usual."

"I'd like to pay for the newlyweds, too," said Mary Ellen. "How much is their tab?"

Gretchen pulled out her pad and flipped through it, "Umm, with tax it's $17.88." She looked at Mary Ellen, "Are you sure? That's awfully nice of you."

Mary Ellen dug around in her purse and came up with three ten-dollar bills. She passed them over to Gretchen, "Don't tell them who paid for it, just tell them it's on the house, okay?"

"Whatever you say, Miss Ellie." Gretchen rang up her order and made change from one of the tens. She placed it with the rest under the tray for later. She glanced at the young couple in number seven, "Do you think that their marriage will last?"

"Who knows?" asked Mary Ellen. "They may one day tell their grandchildren all about the diner in the middle of nowhere that gave them a free breakfast."

Gretchen laughed, "Who knows, indeed." As Mary Ellen turned to leave, she said "Take care, Miss Ellie and I'll see you next month."

"Ciao!" replied Mary Ellen as she exited the door and headed for her car.

* * *

Bert glanced up as the bell over the doorway tinkled merrily. It was the first Friday of the month and he was expecting her arrival, but not until later in the day. He smiled at her as she approached the counter, "Good morning, Miss Ellie. You're a bit earlier than usual."

She returned the smile as she approached the payables window, "Good morning to you, too, Bert." She placed her purse on the counter and proceeded to rummage through it, "I'm early because I want to beat the storm that's coming." She pulled out her invoices for the electricity and water and slid them over to Bert along with the small envelope that contained her payment.

"The Weather Channel says that there's only a ten percent chance of rain today," he said, as he dumped the contents of the envelope and began sorting through the bills and coins.

"Well, the Weather Channel is wrong," she replied.

Bert didn't reply as he added the two bills together and made sure that the total agreed with the cash from the envelope. He removed his rubber stamp from its holder and imprinted the bottom of each statement with PAID IN FULL before tearing off the receipts and passing them back to Miss Ellie. "You can pay your bills online, you know."

She shook her head, "So everyone keeps telling me." She picked up the two slips of paper, slid them into the envelope, and then stuffed it back into her purse. "I've been coming to the Co-Op every month for almost half a century now. I like the physical sensation of exchanging pieces of paper." She smiled at Bert, "Not only do I save on stamps, but it also gives me a chance to see you now and again."

Bert grinned, "You're something else, Miss Ellie." He hemmed and hawed a bit, "Umm, I afraid I won't be seeing you after this."

She looked surprised, "Why is that? Are you quitting your job?"

Bert laughed, shaking his head, "Not exactly, Miss Ellie. I'm retiring next week." He grinned, "I'm moving to Arizona where it's not so humid all of the time."

She snorted, "It may not be humid, but I hear that some parts get up to 120 degrees in the summer."

"They say it's a dry heat," replied Bert.

"The Weather Channel also says ten percent chance of rain today, but they're wrong."

Bert knew better than to argue the point. "The Co-Op's giving me a party next Friday at 5:00pm. You're more than welcome to come." He winked, "There's a rumor that Dinah's cake and cookies might be involved."

"I may take you up on the offer," said Mary Ellen. "But only to see you once more before you go." She shook her head, "I don't want you thinking that I'm only there for the goodies."

"I would never think that of you Miss Ellie." He looked serious, "I'm going to miss you, Mary Ellen. You've been coming in here once a month since I began working here thirty years ago. Other than the occasional encounter around town, I've never really known anything about you." He laughed, "One thing I do know, however, is that you always pay your bills on time."

Mary Ellen blushed slightly, "It's the right thing to do. That's all." She awkwardly reached through the small gap in the window to shake Bert's hand. "I hope you enjoy yourself in Arizona."

"Thanks, Miss Ellie." He released her hand, "Take care, okay?"

"Oh, I will, Bert. Don't you worry about that." She turned and headed out the door, causing the bell to jingle once more.

Bert watched her through the front window as she walked down the sidewalk and out of view. He had no idea how old she was, but she was in far better shape than he was. He didn't know how she managed to keep her little farm going at her age, but she was still sharp as a tack and apparently physically fit enough to plow and harvest her small crops. He patted his beer belly, thinking about his retirement. He thought that he should maybe sign up for a health spa when he got settled into Sun City. Turning to his computer screen, he began browsing the available places in northwest Phoenix.

* * *

The first Friday of the month was also shopping day for Mary Ellen. She pulled into the lot of the feedstore and drove around to the rear where she backed her Bel Air up to the dock. As she got out of her car, she was greeted by Willy, "Good morning, Miss Ellie. You're here a bit earlier than usual."

"A fine morning, indeed, but we're in for a storm this afternoon," she said, as she walked around to the back of her car. "I have things I need to tend to before it hits."

"The weatherman on the radio says it's going to be partly cloudy with a slight chance of showers."

She unlocked the trunk with her key and lifted the heavy lid, "He been wrong before, you know." She reached up and grabbed the bag of corn meal from Willy and placed it in the trunk.

"Well, if you say it's going to rain, then it's going to rain," he agreed, as he handed her another bag of ground kernels.

She hefted the bag into the trunk and closed the lid, "A real downpour, I'm afraid. You saw the sky this morning."

He nodded, "True enough." He looked down at Mary Ellen, "You doing okay, Miss Ellie?"

She smiled, "Of course I am, Willy." She looked around, "Looks like you're doing okay as well. How much do I owe you?"

"People always have to feed their animals, you know." He handed her a receipt, already stamped PAID IN FULL to save time. "Total comes to $15.95."

She opened the door to her car and leaned in to dig through her purse. She walked back to the dock and handed him some bills, "Here's $16.00, Willy." She grinned, "You can keep the change."

Willy acted overwhelmed for her benefit, "OMG! I can't believe what a big tipper you are!"

Mary Ellen knew what OMG meant. She didn't have a cell phone or internet connection, but she kept up with the times. Laughing out loud, she replied, "LOL, Willy." She slid onto the bench seat of her car and closed the door. Waving goodbye, she drove off and circled around the building to the highway.

* * *

As she pulled up in front of the post office, she marveled at the sleek modern building plopped down between the dry goods store and the bakery. No matter how bad times might be, there always seemed to be enough money to periodically refurbish this building. She remembered when it was a simple wooden structure with one clerk. Today it was a mostly empty tile expanse with self-service everything and stations for three clerks. She entered the empty lobby and noted that, as usual, two of the stations were closed, so she walked up to the one in the center. The young girl behind the counter was obviously new here since Mary Ellen had never seen her before.

"Good morning, ma'am," said the clerk. "How may I help you?"

"I'm here to pick up my mail," answered Mary Ellen. "It's RFD number 2."

"Oh, that's already out for delivery, ma'am."

Mary Ellen frowned, "It's the first Friday of the month."

The young woman looked confused, "Why, I guess it is, isn't it?"

"Yes, it is. And you're supposed to hold my mail for will call."

Somewhat flustered, the clerk replied, "I have no idea what you're talking about." She pointed, "If you want to come and pick it up yourself, you'll need to rent one of the P.O. boxes."

Mary Ellen counted to ten before replying, "I've been getting my mail here since long before you were ever born. I've always picked it up on the first Friday of the month. I also save your couriers the trouble of daily deliveries and voluntarily reduced the service to only once a week."

"Umm, let me go get Tracy and see if she knows anything about it." She quickly disappeared through a doorway in the back.

Mary Ellen shook her head. "*The world is going to Hell in a handbasket,*" she thought to herself. She gave a small laugh as she realized that she had been saying that for most of her life now. The world was changing right before her eyes and she didn't like most of it. Her thoughts were interrupted by the return of the clerk followed by another woman.

"Hello, ma'am, my name is Tracy. Amber tells me that there's some confusion about your delivery?"

"Where's Ted?" asked Mary Ellen. "Or Kerry?"

"They've been rotated out to Atlanta and we've been brought in as replacements." Tracy smiled, "I'm sorry to see that we're obviously off to a bad start with one of our customers." She reached across the counter, "I'm Tracy Cervantes and you are ...?"

Mary Ellen shook her hand, "I'm Mary Ellen McDouglas. RFD 2." Letting go, she continued, "But please call me Miss Ellie. That's what everyone else does."

"Well, Miss Ellie. What seems to be the problem?" asked Tracy.

"I get my mail delivered every Friday, except for the first Friday of each month. That's when I come to town and do my shopping and pay my bills. And, since I'm already here, I save you folks the trouble of delivering the mail all the way out to my farm."

Tracy nodded, "I understand. That also explains the weird post-a-note that simply said *'First Friday H2'* on it. Now I get it. Hold RFD 2 on the first Friday." She shook her head apologetically, "I had no idea what it meant so I tossed it out." She smiled, "Now that we've got that straightened out, we'll make sure to hold it for you from now on."

"Well, thank you, Tracy. And Amber. It's nice to make your acquaintance. And welcome to our little town."

Amber laughed, "It's not quite what we're used to, but we're adapting."

"That's good to hear. It's either adapt or die," replied Mary Ellen. "Since I'm here anyway, I need some stamps."

Amber pointed, "You can get those at the self-service machines over there."

"I want them in sheets. I collect the corner blocks." She looked at the bank of machines, "Those don't dispense sheets."

"Not a problem, Miss Ellie," assured Tracy. "What stamps did you have in mind?"

"There's a new issue with a variety of herons on them. Just issued last month." She looked hopeful, "I don't suppose you have any yet?"

"Let's take a look," said Tracy, as she logged into the terminal on the counter. "We got the latest batch last week. As far as I know, no one else has bothered to purchase any." She smiled at Mary Ellen, "I'll go and fetch them for you." She disappeared through the doorway behind the counter.

Mary Ellen looked at Amber, "She's very helpful, you know."

"Yes, ma'am," she replied, not missing the implication.

She was saved from further embarrassment by Tracy's return. "We have a dozen of the new heron series," she said, as she laid the stack on the counter. "How many do you want?"

Mary Ellen glanced at them and confirmed they were the ones she wanted. "I'll take all of them," she said, as she opened up her purse. "How much are they?"

If Tracy was surprised, she didn't show it. "Let's see ... at ten dollars a sheet, that comes to 120 dollars."

Amber asked, helpfully, "Did you want to pay that with credit or debit?"

"With cash, actually." Mary Ellen hauled out a sheaf of twenties and counted them out onto the counter. There were exactly six of them.

Tracy raised an eyebrow at this, but rang up the transaction. She placed the cash in the drawer before handing the printed receipt to Mary Ellen. "Here you go,

Miss Ellie." She slid the sheets forward. "Is there anything else I can help you with?"

Mary Ellen shook her head as she picked up the stamps, "No, Tracy, that pretty much takes care of it." She smiled at Amber and then at Tracy, "I must say that you've been very helpful, Tracy." She folded the sheets carefully into quarters and put them in her purse. "I'll see you folks in a month or so." She turned and crossed the tile lobby, exiting the front door of the Post Office.

"What an odd lady," said Amber.

"I didn't think so," replied Tracy. "Why do you say that?"

"You heard her. She only gets delivery on Fridays. How does anyone go a week without getting their mail?"

"Maybe she does everything online?"

"Then why buy stamps?" pointed out Amber. "She said that she drives into town to pay her bills."

"Which she apparently pays with cash." Tracy laughed, "Welcome to nowhere, Amber. Like the lady said, adapt or die."

* * *

Mary Ellen skipped the dry goods store and the pharmacy and decided that she would hit them next time around. She had more than enough supplies to tide her over until then. However, the broken bolt on her tractor couldn't wait. She pulled into an angled parking slot in front of the hardware store and went inside where Thom welcomed her, "Good morning, Miss Ellie."

"Good morning, Thom. How's business?"

"Not bad, considering." He smiled, "What can I do for you? Do you need some more caulking?"

"Actually, I need a five-eighths bolt. Coarse thread, three-quarters of an inch long."

"Let's go take a look," he said, as he led the way to the back of the store. Walking along the rows of cabinets full of fasteners and miscellany, he stopped and pulled out one of the trays. Mary Ellen peered around him as he told her what she could already see for herself, "I got a half-inch and a one-inch. I don't have a three-quarters."

"I'll take the one-inch," she told him. "I'll just cut it to size."

"Okay, then." Thom placed the bolt in a little paper envelope. "Need anything else?"

"Yes. I need some more D cells." She led the way to the display of batteries and picked out a six-pack. She turned to Thom, "I think that'll do it."

She followed him to the register by the front door and waited as he rang up the two items. "$1.37 for the bolt and $7.35 for the batteries ... with tax it comes to $9.42." He placed her purchase in a bag as she dove into her purse. She fished out a ten and handed it to him. "Anything else you need?" he asked, as he counted out her change.

"Nope, I'm good," she said, picking up the bag and then heading for the door.

"Take care," he called out after her.

She looked back over her shoulder, "You, too, Thom."

He watched through the front window as she opened the door to her Bel Air and climbed inside. As she backed out of the spot, he imagined what her car would look like if she ever got it properly restored. He often teased her about it, but she said it wasn't important what things looked like on the outside, but what they truly were on the inside. He shook his head and headed to the back room to order some more of the five-eighths by three-quarter inch bolts before he forgot about them. He really needed to take a complete inventory to assess his stock. "*Maybe this weekend,*" he thought to himself, but in his heart, he knew it wasn't going to happen.

* * *

Mary Ellen carefully backed her car into the garage. Turning off the engine, she got out and opened up the trunk. As she leaned in and picked up one of the feed bags, she thought about how easily she used to heft a hundred-pound bag with no problem. Several years ago, she'd had Willy start giving her two fifty-pounders instead. As she placed the bag against the wall and turned to get the other one, she thought that maybe it was time to get four twenty-five-pounders instead. She set the second bag down next to the first and then shut the trunk lid. Retrieving her purse from the front seat, she closed the car door and went into the kitchen. Setting her purse down on the counter, she stood in front of the sink and looked out of the window at the darkening sky. She went back outside through the still open garage door and headed for the barn. Along the way, hoping to get her attention, she repeatedly yelled, "Yo, Bessie, yo!" She didn't think that it would help and it turned out that she was right. She waited for about ten minutes by the barn door until the first raindrops started to fall. Bessie wasn't terribly smart, but she knew to come in out of the rain. Sure enough, she came running in from the field ahead of the pelting drops. As she entered the barn, a bright bolt of lightning flickered which was followed a few seconds later by a low rumble in the distance. The dairy cow needed no further urging and sought sanctuary in her stall. Mary Ellen closed the stall door and then dragged the main door shut, making sure it was securely fastened. The rain was starting to really come down now and she ran the whole way back to the garage, getting fairly soaked in the process. As she pulled the door down, she looked out at the downpour and nodded to herself, "*Slight chance of rain, my ass.*" Her joints were never wrong.

Raising Miss Ellie

Chapter Two

The old woman sat behind her desk and glared at the two men seated in the wingback chairs facing her. She looked from one to the other, her dissatisfaction and irritation clearly displayed. She focused on the man on her right, "You had one job, Michael. To make sure that he didn't get away."

"Yes, Mum. Please don't blame Luke. I take full responsibility."

"Well, that's a given. You had no business letting him do the job instead of yourself." She turned to the other hapless individual, "What exactly happened, Luke?"

"I was watching him, not ten feet away, when I heard Peter yelling for help."

"He's an accomplished ventriloquist, you know."

"Yes, I know that now, Mum. I ran to find Peter who told me that he hadn't yelled for me. By the time I got back he had vanished." He looked glum, "I searched the immediate area for a few minutes and then alerted Michael."

Michael spoke up, "I've put out an APB for him. It's been less than an hour since he disappeared and I expect that we'll find him soon enough."

The old woman shook her head, "Don't underestimate his resourcefulness." She looked from one to the other, "When we find him and bring him back, let's try not to let this happen again, okay?"

"Yes, Mum," the two replied in unison.

She sighed, "You're dismissed. Let me know when you have an update on him."

"Will do, Mum," replied Michael, as the two men stood and quickly left the room.

The woman turned and looked out the window, "Wherever you are, my dear, we'll find you, eventually."

Chapter Three

Mary Ellen awoke with a start. It had still been raining when she went to bed, but it had obviously stopped since then. She glanced at the glow-in-the-dark hands on her clock and saw that it was nearly midnight. She lay quietly, listening, wondering what might have caused her to awaken so suddenly. After a few moments, she heard the murmuring of the chickens as they were disturbed by something. They quieted right back down, but she knew that something was in the henhouse. She quietly pulled back the covers and got out of bed. She grabbed her galoshes and slid her naked feet into them. She felt for the double-barreled shotgun that was leaning against the nightstand. Pushing the release lever, she broke open the action and felt to make sure that there were shells in both chambers. Rock salt on the right and double-ought buckshot on the left. She knew that they were there, but it never hurt to check. She held the release as she eased the action shut without a sound. She grabbed her Maglite from the nightstand and headed for the den. She opened the door and eased her way onto the porch where she stopped to listen again. The clucking started up once more and she headed toward the henhouse without making a sound. The gate to the pen was ajar and she quietly stepped in front of the open door to the coop. Cradling the shotgun in her right arm, she turned on the Maglite. She was expecting to find a raccoon or a possum, but what was caught in the spotlight was a young boy. He tried to shield his eyes from the glare with his arm as Mary Ellen stared at him in surprise. About four-and-a-half feet tall, he looked to be about nine or ten years old and, at first, she thought he was Hispanic based on his black hair and skin color. However, as he moved his arm, the shadows on his cheekbones suggested that maybe he was Native American. When he finally lowered his arm and looked at her properly, she saw his eyes and wondered if perhaps he was Asian. With a start, she realized that he was soaking wet and shivering, either from the cold or fear or, more than likely, both. Lowering her gun, she asked gently, "Do you speak English?"

"Yes, ma'am. I do."

"What are you doing in my henhouse?"

"I came to steal some eggs, ma'am." He looked ashamed, "I know it's wrong, ma'am, but I'm starving and miserable and didn't know what else to do."

Mary Ellen shook her head, "Do you prefer your eggs raw? Or cooked?"

"It doesn't matter. The eggs provide protein either way."

She laughed, "Come with me and let's get you dried off and cleaned up. I know you're hungry, but you're not eating at my table until you're presentable."

"Yes, ma'am." He meekly followed her as she led the way back to the house.

"My name's Mary Ellen, but you can call me Miss Ellie." She looked back at him, "What's your name?"

"It's Miguel, but I prefer to be called Mig."

The back door was still ajar and she pushed it fully open, flipping on the light-switch as she did so. "Come on in, Mig. I won't bite." The boy stepped cautiously into the room and looked around. Mary Ellen shut the door behind him, "Come with me and I'll start the tub running while you get out of those wet clothes." Just outside the bathroom, she opened the cupboard and removed a large beach towel, and handed it to Mig. "Here, hold onto this while I get the water running." He followed her into the bathroom and watched as she sat on the edge of the tub and turned on the taps. "That'll take a little bit to warm up." She stood and looked down at the small child. "Do you know how to take a bath? Use soap? Scrub behind the ears?"

He smiled, "Yes, ma'am, I know all about personal hygiene."

She seemed satisfied with his answer. "Okay, then, I'm going to go fix you something to eat. I don't have any clothes that will fit you, but I'll leave a robe hanging on the door. It'll have to do until we can figure out something better for you."

"Yes, ma'am." He smiled again, "Thank you for your kindness, Miss Ellie. I don't know how I will ever be able to repay you."

"Don't you be worrying about that, young man." She gestured at the tub, "Holler if you need anything." She closed the door behind her and went to find her old robe. She returned and hung it on the doorknob to the bathroom before going into the kitchen and warming up the hotplate. She had many questions for young Mig, but they could wait until he had eaten and felt more comfortable around her. She had no idea where he came from or how he came to be in the middle of nowhere, but she would find out soon enough.

***

Thirty minutes later, Mary Ellen sat across the small table in her kitchen, watching Mig finish off his second plate of scrambled eggs. She wished that she had something else on hand with which to feed him, but he seemed more than satisfied with what she had prepared. She watched as he drained the glass of milk and set it back on the table. His manners clearly indicated an honest upbringing and Mary Ellen was dying to learn all about him. "Would you like some more?" she asked.

He smiled shyly, "No, Miss Ellie. That was the most wonderful meal that I've ever had." He rubbed his stomach, "No, ma'am. I'm think I'm full now."

"Well, then. It's nigh on one o'clock in the morning and way past our bedtime, I think." She pushed back her chair and stood, "I would imagine that you could use some sleep about now." She yawned, "I know that I can." She looked down at the small lad, "Come with me and we'll get you settled into the extra bedroom."

Mig pushed back his own chair and stood to face her, "I think I'd best be moving on, Miss Ellie." He rubbed his stomach again, "I really appreciate your kindness, but it's time for me to go."

"Go where?" She frowned at Mig, "Where are your parents?"

"I don't have any," he replied.

"Well, then, who's your guardian? You must have somebody to take care of you?"

He snorted, "They're the ones that I'm running away from."

Mary Ellen wasn't sure what to make of this. Or what to do, for that matter. Maybe he had abusive foster parents? Or maybe he was part of some sex trade? She had read in Reader's Digest all about the horrible things that happened to children who fell into the hands of evil people. "Why are you running from them?"

He looked down, "They make me do things for them. Chores, they call them."

Chores? Mary Ellen's imagination ran wild with possible things he might have been made to do. "What sort of chores?"

"Just things." He looked up at her, his face betraying his fear, "Please don't tell anyone, Miss Ellie. I don't want them to find me."

She looked down at his feet, still barefoot like she had found him. "Look at yourself. You have no shoes. You're in my old bathrobe." She shook her head, "No, Mig. You need to get some sleep before you make any rash decisions. You're not in any shape to go traipsing around the countryside in the dark of night." She reached out and took his small hand with her own. "You're safe here with me, for the time being. I don't have a phone and, even if I did, there's no point in trying to contact the authorities around here on a weekend." He allowed her to lead him to the spare bedroom where she turned down the covers and found him one of Henry's old shirts to use as a nightshirt of sorts. "I'm going to leave the hall light on for you in case you need to get up and go potty." Mig looked up at her from the bed, his gratitude clearly showing on his face. He looked so sweet and innocent and Mary Ellen impulsively leaned down and gave him a quick kiss on the forehead. "Goodnight my little Mig." She pulled the covers up a bit, "I'll see you in the morning, okay?"

"Okay, Miss Ellie." He smiled, "Thanks again for everything you've done for me." He gave a yawn, "I'll see you in the morning."

Raising Miss Ellie

Chapter Four

Mary Ellen woke up a little later than usual. By the time she got to Bessie, the cow was beginning to complain. Living on a farm had certain necessary rituals that followed the sun, which waited for no man. Or woman, in Mary Ellen's case. By the time she had finished, the sun was fully up and she went to check on Mig, who was still asleep in the spare room. She went into the kitchen and began to fix breakfast for the two of them. She was going to have to find something else for Mig besides eggs and milk. There was a time when they had an abundance of pork, but she had quit raising hogs when her brother Henry passed away some twenty years earlier. Beneath her, in the root cellar, there were countless jars of canned vegetables, but nothing that would normally be part of a breakfast. She sighed. *"What am I going to do with him?"* she asked herself. She cracked four eggs into the small frying pan and stirred them with her spatula. In only a few minutes, they were ready and she scraped them onto a plate. She took the milk pail from the refrigerator and stirred in the cream that had risen to the top again before pouring some into the two glasses. She was planning to go rouse Mig when he walked into the kitchen, still dressed in Henry's old shirt. She suppressed a laugh at the sight—

the shirt hung on him like a tent, well below his knees. "Well, good morning, Mig," she said. "I was just coming to get you."

He smiled at her, "Good morning, Miss Ellie." He pulled out the chair and sat down at the table, "Did you get enough sleep? I was worried that my arrival had an adverse effect on your sleeping pattern."

Mary Ellen was a bit surprised by how he had phrased his question. "Yes, Mig, your arrival certainly impacted my sleeping pattern." She smiled, "However, I got up a little later than usual and I'll just go to bed a little earlier than usual. No harm done." She sat down across from him and noticed that he waited until she was ready to eat before starting to do so himself. Once more, she was impressed with his manners. Wherever he came from, they must have at least been civilized enough to teach him properly. "So, Mig, where are you from?"

He finished chewing before replying, "I'm not really sure."

She looked at him, "How can you not know where you lived?"

"I don't want to go back," he said, somewhat sullenly. "Therefore, it doesn't matter from whence I came."

Mary Ellen decided to try another tack, "How long ago did you run away?"

"I'm not really sure," he replied, as he forked another bite of eggs into his mouth.

"*This is getting me nowhere*," thought Mary Ellen. She said nothing further and ate her eggs in silence. When she was finished, she was pleasantly surprised when Mig stood up and began clearing the table. She sat and watched him and wondered what made him tick. He carefully rinsed the plates and glasses and then proceeded to scrub the frying pan. She pushed her chair back and stood up, "I think we need to make you an outfit to wear. Something that fits you a little better."

Mig placed the frying pan in the drying rack and turned to her, "How would you do that?"

She laughed, "I have an old Singer sewing machine that can turn out pretty much anything."

Mig dried his hands and carefully hung the towel back on its hook. "I would like to see this machine that can make new clothes."

Mary Ellen shook her head. Imagine never having seen anyone sew before. "Come with me and I'll show you how we're going to make you a jumpsuit out of denim." She looked down at his bare feet, "What happened to your shoes?"

"I must have lost them somewhere," admitted Mig.

She sighed, "I think I have a pair of moccasins somewhere that were a gift from a friend. They were way too small for me, but I'll bet that they would fit you." She left the kitchen for the den, "Once we have something you can wear in public, we're going to take a drive into town."

Mig held back, "I can't go anywhere in public." He looked dismayed, "They'll find me for sure."

"I'll have to come up with some sort of explanation for your presence, but no one's going to find you around here." She laughed, "You can count on that."

Mig didn't look so sure, "You don't know these people. They have their spies everywhere."

"I hardly doubt that they're going to find you where we're going." She shook her head, "You're just going to have to trust me on this, okay?"

Mig hesitated a moment before replying, "Okay, Miss Ellie. I trust you." He followed her into the den where she dragged her sewing machine out of the closet and began to set it up.

* * *

As they drove along the highway, Mary Ellen kept glancing at Mig. She was pleased with the jumper she had made him and the moccasins fit him like a glove. He sat quietly and looked at everything as they drove along. "A penny for your thoughts, young man."

He looked at her, "I was just thinking about how beautiful everything is here." He smiled, "You're lucky to live here, Miss Ellie."

"I guess I am, Mig." She shook her head, "When I was your age, I thought I might get to see all the sights of the world one day."

"What sights would those be?"

She thought for a moment, "Well, you know, like going to Paris to see the Eiffel Tower. Or New York where there's the Statue of Liberty. Or maybe Egypt where they have the pyramids."

"I take it that you never got your wish," said Mig.

She laughed, "No, Mig, I never did. But I *did* get to go to Memphis several times for a trade convention." She smiled, "I was born and raised right here on the farm. Somehow, I just never got around to leaving it."

"You seem happy enough, Miss Ellie."

Changing the subject, she said, "How about you, Mig. What do you want to be when you grow up?"

"Older than I am now," he replied solemnly.

She laughed, "No, seriously. If you could do anything you wanted, what would it be?"

He sat quietly for a few long moments, obviously thinking about it. Finally, he looked at her, "I think I'd like to go to a carnival and ride the rides. To eat cake and ice cream and cotton candy. To ride a bicycle down the lane. To build a snowman and make snow angels in the snow. To ride a skateboard and fly a kite. To swing on a rope and jump into a creek."

She grinned, "Is that all?"

He shook his head, "No, but it's a good start, at least."

She glanced at him, "You've never done any of these things before?"

"No, ma'am."

Mary Ellen was taken aback by this. How could anyone raise a child and not let them do any of the normal things a child did when growing up? "What exactly have you done up until now? What did your foster parents make you do?"

"For as long as I can remember, they've treated me as an adult. I happen to have a rather unique skillset that they need." He laughed, "No, in their minds, there's no place for my being a child."

Mary Ellen was intrigued by this. "What sort of skillset?" she asked.

Raising Miss Ellie

"Do you know what a prodigy is, Miss Ellie?"

"Well, of course." She looked at him, "Is that what you are? Some sort of child prodigy?"

"Not exactly." He shook his head, "Do you know what an idiot savant is?"

She looked at him again, "Yes, but you don't strike me as some sort of Rain Man or something."

"Rainman?" he asked, clearly puzzled.

"You know, like in the movie with Dustin Hoffman?"

He shook his head again, "I've never watched a movie before. I think I'll add that to my list of things I'd like to do." Mary Ellen sat quietly digesting this. She wasn't quite sure how to respond. Prodigy? Idiot savant? Mig pointed to the dashboard, "Does that thing tell you how fast we're going?"

"You mean the speedometer?"

"Yes. If I understand it correctly, it says that our relative land speed is ninety miles per hour."

Mary Ellen smiled, "Well, that's one way of putting it."

"But that sign back there clearly said the limit was sixty-five miles per hour." He looked at her, "Our current velocity is in excess of that by nearly thirty-eight-and-a-half percent."

She laughed at this, "I live thirty miles outside of town. If I drove the speed limit, it would take a lot longer to get there." She swung her arm in an arc, "There's nothing but farmland around here. There's only one sheriff in the county and he's either too busy or too lazy to bother with pulling me over for speeding."

Mig didn't respond to this, but sat quietly staring out at the countryside as it whizzed by at ninety miles per hour.

* * *

It was almost noon by the time they arrived on the outskirts of the town and Mary Ellen thought they should start with lunch at Dinah's. She pulled into a vacant parking spot and turned off the engine. She looked at Mig, "Okay, here's the deal. You're technically my great-nephew on my brother's side. His wife left him for another man so it would stand to reason there would be some remote relation." She looked thoughtful, "They sent you to live here for the summer so that you could learn all about farming."

"That makes you my great-aunt, right?"

She smiled at how quickly he caught on. "Yes, but the less said about where you came from the better."

"I got it, Miss Ellie." He opened the passenger door and got out, closing it behind him.

"*Here goes nothing,*" thought Mary Ellen, as she got out and joined him. He casually reached out to take her hand and she grasped it firmly as they walked to the door. Like yesterday, her favorite booth in the back was empty and she led Mig to it and sat down. She had caught the looks from several of the other customers out of the corner of her eye. She had been unwilling to look at them directly, but knew they were wondering who Mig was.

"Well, hello Miss Ellie," said Gretchen, as she placed a cup of coffee on the table in front of Mary Ellen. "What brings you back into town so soon?" She looked at Mig and raised an eyebrow.

"This is my great-nephew, Mig. It's short for Miguel." She smiled, "He's going to be staying with me for the summer to learn all about farming."

"You never said anything about it," replied Gretchen.

"It plum slipped my mind. As a matter of fact, when his parents pulled up in that storm last night, I greeted them with my shotgun." She laughed, "We got Mig settled in and then they left at the crack of dawn to go home again."

"Where are you from, Mig?" asked Gretchen.

"They live in New Orleans," interjected Mary Ellen.

Gretchen smiled, "I've been there before. For Mardi Gras." She turned to Mary Ellen, "I'm not really sure what you want, Miss Ellie. It's a bit late in the day for your usual." She handed her a menu and then proffered one to Mig, "I'll give you a few minutes to figure out what you want." She pointed to the coffee, "Should I leave this? Or take it?"

"No, no. Leave it," said Mary Ellen. "I need the caffeine."

"Okay then," said Gretchen, as she headed back to the kitchen.

"What do you usually have for lunch?" Mary Ellen asked.

"Our bodies need nutrients. These can take many forms."

She shook her head, "Yes, but what do you like?"

"I want to try the blueberry pancakes with maple syrup and butter," he answered.

Mary Ellen got the impression that he had never had them before. "I think I'll have the chicken salad sandwich and a glass of cold milk."

Mig continued to study the menu until Gretchen returned to take their order. "So, lady and gent, what'll it be?"

"I'll have the chicken salad sandwich and a glass of milk, please."

"Whole-wheat or white bread?"

"White bread, of course."

"Anything else?"

"No, just that."

Gretchen turned to Mig, "And what can we get for you, young man?"

Mig looked up from the menu, "I'd like three blueberry pancakes with butter and maple syrup. Orange juice to drink, and a side of onion rings, please."

She smiled at his order, "Anything else?"

"No, ma'am. That's all."

Gretchen grabbed the two menus, "I'll be right back with your milk and OJ." She left them to go fetch the drinks.

* * *

Mary Ellen thought that the sandwich was quite good, but while she was eating, she was distracted by watching Mig as he dug into his pancakes and syrup. And his onion rings. He poured a liberal amount of syrup on everything and she was beginning to worry about the effect of so much sugar. "How old are you, Mig?"

He finished chewing his bite of onion ring before answering, "I'm not really sure." He saw her look, "Birthdays were not on the agenda while I was growing up. Every day was another day filled with work. There was always so much that needed to be done."

Mary Ellen almost choked on her chicken salad, "Surely you had the weekends off? Didn't you ever go on a vacation?"

He shook his head, "Not for as long as I can remember." He grinned at her, "I always wanted a vacation and I think I'm finally on one right now!"

"What sort of monsters are these foster parents?" wondered Mary Ellen. As she watched Mig clean his plate of food, she made up her mind, right then and there. If his foster parents ever showed up to take him home again, she would fight them tooth and nail to prevent it. From what little she had heard from Mig and what she could only imagine left no room for doubt.

Gretchen approached the booth, "My, my, you must have been hungry." She smiled at Mig, "Did you leave any room for dessert?"

He returned the smile, "Yes, ma'am, I did." He looked at Mary Ellen, "Is it okay if I get a hot fudge sundae?"

"Of course, it is. As long as you don't mind me having some of it."

"I'll make it a little bigger than usual, with two spoons, okay?" She pointed to the plates, "Can I get those out of your way?"

"Yes," replied Mary Ellen. "I think we're done eating." She smiled at Gretchen, "Your chicken salad sandwich is almost as good as my own."

"I'll take that as a compliment, Miss Ellie. Thank you!" She gathered the plates and balanced one on another and left to return them to the kitchen.

"I don't believe that I've had a hot fudge sundae in maybe twenty years," said Mary Ellen.

Mig grinned, "I've never had one before. Are they good?"

"You do know that you've had a severely deprived childhood? Don't you?"

"I know that it hasn't been like most childhoods, but deprived?" He smiled, "Do you know what Asperger's syndrome is, Miss Ellie?"

"It's a type of autism, as I recall." She looked at him, "Why do you ask these things? I'm willing to go along with the child prodigy thing, but you don't seem to fit the others."

She looked up as Gretchen approached with their dessert. "Here you go." She looked at Mig, "You have to eat it before the fudge cools, you know."

"I knew that," he said, as he eagerly picked up his spoon. He waited for Mary Ellen to pick up hers.

"Thanks, Gretchen." She looked at the sundae, "That's a healthy portion you gave us. I hope we can finish it!"

She laughed, "Oh, I have a feeling Mig will make sure that none of it goes to waste." She left to attend to another patron.

Mary Ellen noticed that Mig was waiting for her. "*Such polite manners*," she thought to herself.

"What are the two red things on top?" asked Mig.

Mary Ellen was surprised by his question. Had this poor boy never even seen a cherry? Or a picture of one? "These are cherries, Mig." She picked one up, "You put the whole thing in your mouth and then pull out the stem." She demonstrated the process.

He picked up the other cherry and did the same. Smiling, he said, "Cherries are really good, Miss Ellie."

"Yes, they certainly are." She picked up her spoon and said, "Now we can dig into the sundae." She watched with amusement as he scooped a liberal amount into his mouth. The expressions that crossed his face were such joyous simple ones. She wished that she could feel like that again. She took a small scoop with her own spoon and placed it in her mouth. The battle between hot and cold fought it out on her tongue and she realized that she had forgotten how good the sensation was. She took a larger portion and repeated the process. She noticed Mig watching her with equal amusement. "What?" she asked.

"It's simply amazing, isn't it?"

She laughed, "Yes, Mig, it certainly is." She scooped another bite out of the dessert.

* * *

When they finally finished, they slid out of the booth and walked to the front to pay their bill. Along the way, everyone smiled and nodded at Mig as if they knew him. Gretchen approached the cash register, "I hope you didn't mind me telling everyone about Mig." She looked apologetic, "They were all asking about him, of course."

Mary Ellen smiled, "I saw the looks we were getting. I appreciate you putting everyone's curiosity to rest."

She put her purse on the counter, "How much do I owe you for this extravagant lunch we had today?"

Gretchen pulled her pad from her pocket and found the tab. She pulled it out totaled it up. "It comes to $14.74."

"$15.74, ma'am," said Mig.

Gretchen looked down at him and then retotaled the ticket. "By golly, he's right, Miss Ellie! I forgot to carry a one." She looked back at Mig, "How did you do that?"

"I've got a knack for numbers, that's all."

Mary Ellen looked thoughtful, "How much is 427 times 394, Mig?"

"168,238."

Gretchen looked at Mary Ellen, "Is that right?"

"How would I know? Do I look like a calculator?" replied Mary Ellen.

In answer, Gretchen reached under the counter and pulled one out. She glanced at Mig, "How much is 588 ... times ... 766?" As she said this, she was punching the numbers into the calculator.

"450,408."

Gretchen held the calculator so that Mary Ellen could see it. She looked at Mig again, "How did you do that?"

"I don't really know. The numbers just pop into my head." He smiled, "Like I said, I have a knack for numbers."

Gretchen shook her head, "That's not a knack, Mig. That's a gift."

Mary Ellen agreed. She waved a twenty-dollar bill in front of Gretchen to get her attention. "This should cover our bill and the rest is yours for making Mig's first encounter with a hot fudge sundae such a memorable one."

"Why, thank you, Miss Ellie," she said, as she opened the register and made change for the bill before tossing the rest into the tip jar. She looked down at Mig, "It was a real pleasure having you here, Mig." She glanced at Mary Ellen, "You make sure that she brings you back from time to time, okay?"

He grinned, "Yes, ma'am, I will."

Mary Ellen reached down and took his hand, "Thanks again, Gretchen. We'll be back sooner than later, I promise." She turned and held the door open for Mig and followed him through the opening.

* * *

Penny greeted them as they entered the clothing store, "Good afternoon, Miss Ellie. What brings you to town on a Saturday?" She looked at Mig, "And who is this adorable child that you have with you?"

"Hello, Penny. It's good to see you again." She turned, "This is my great-nephew, Mig. He's here for the summer to learn farming from me." She looked at Penny, "He's the reason we're here. Is Gerald around?"

"He's in the back. I'll go get him for you." She turned and headed to the rear of the store.

Mig was looking around at the racks of jackets and dresses, "There's so many different ones. Why would you need so many of them?"

Mary Ellen laughed, "When we have time, I'll tell you all about the fashion industry." She frowned, "Please don't tell me that the only clothes you've ever had were like that horrid gown I found you in?" His lack of a reply was an answer in itself. "*Monsters!*" she thought bitterly.

"Miss Ellie!" cried Gerald in his booming voice as he emerged from the back of the store with Penny. He walked up and shook her hand. "It's good to see you!" He turned to Mig, "And this must be Mig," he said, stooping down slightly to shake his hand as well. "Welcome to Klinemann's!"

Mary Ellen always laughed at his exuberance. "We need some appropriate clothing for my great-nephew here. Something he can play in and something he can work in."

"I see," said Gerald. He beckoned, "Come this way and let me show you what we have in his size." He led the way to the side of the store that had clothing for young boys. "First we need to see what size you are." He had Mig stand on a short stool as he measured his waist and inseam. He went over to a rack and sorted through it, pulling out two different pairs of pants to try on. He handed them to Mary Ellen, "Have him try these on, okay?"

Mary Ellen took them, but hesitated. "He needs some underwear first, I think." She looked at him apologetically, "His parents didn't send him with much in the way of clothing. I had to improvise, I'm afraid."

Gerald nodded, "I understand." He walked over to the underwear section and picked up a three-pack in the right size. He returned and handed them to Mary Ellen. "These are what they call tighty whities. They should do the trick." He looked at Mig, "I suspect that he'll be needing socks and shoes as well." He pointed to the changing rooms, "Put on the undies and try on these two pairs of pants. Once I get an idea of the fit, we can go from there."

Mig looked at Mary Ellen who took him by the hand and led him into the changing area. She opened the pack of underwear and handed him a pair along with the two pairs of jeans. "Go into that room there and take off all of your clothes. Put these on and leave them on. They're yours now. Then put on one of these pair of jeans and come back out. I'll be waiting right here for you."

He nodded, "Okay, Miss Ellie." He pulled back the curtain and entered the changing room, closing the curtain behind him.

Sitting down on the small chair in the waiting room, Mary Ellen was afforded a view of Mig's feet that were visible below the curtain. She watched as he removed his moccasins and then the jumper she had made for him hit the floor. As he started to put the underwear on backwards, she almost said something, but he figured it out on his own. In another moment or so, he pulled back the curtain and walked stiffly out into the waiting area. He was shirtless, but seemed indifferent to the fact.

"Well, Miss Ellie? What do you think?"

She studied the pants, "Those look like they fit you quite well. Are they comfortable?"

"There not as comfortable as your jumper."

She laughed, "They need to be washed first." She pointed to the changing room, "Go back and put on the other pair and let's see if that's any better."

He nodded and disappeared back into the changing room again. A couple of minutes later he re-emerged. "I think that these are a little long, Miss Ellie."

She agreed, "Yes, they are, Mig." She stood, "Go back and get dressed in your jumper again. Don't forget to leave the underwear on. When you're done, bring the pants with you back to where we got them."

"Yes, ma'am," he replied and entered the changing room once more.

Mary Ellen left the waiting room and found Gerald waiting for them. "The one pair's too long, but the other is just right."

"Ah, very good." He proceeded to pick two more hangers off the rack. "I think that three pairs of jeans, three work-shirts, six pairs of socks, and two pairs of shoes would be appropriate."

Mary Ellen frowned, "He needs all of that?"

"Well, you could probably get by with only two pairs of jeans, I suppose. But a boy needs fresh socks each day."

She nodded, "How about two pairs of pants, three shirts, and seven pairs of socks? He likes the moccasins so we'll skip the shoes for now."

"But of course. You can have whatever you want, Miss Ellie." He turned as Mig emerged from the changing area, "If you'll just hand me those pants, Mig, I think that you're all done here." Mig complied and Gerald set them on the rack before leading them to the front of the store where the register was located. Penny tallied up the total, "That comes to $415.27, Miss Ellie."

"I don't have that much cash on me, I'm afraid," confessed Mary Ellen. "If you don't mind waiting, I'll just run down the street to the bank."

Gerald smiled, "There's no need to do that, Miss Ellie. Go ahead and take the clothes and we'll send you a bill at the end of the month."

"Are you sure?" asked Mary Ellen.

"Of course," said Gerald. "You've been a customer of this establishment since my grandfather first opened it." He handed Mig the two shopping bags with his new clothes. "I hope you enjoy these, young man."

"I'm sure that I will," replied Mig. "Especially the underwear. It's very comfy." Gerald chuckled in response.

"We'd best be going," said Mary Ellen. "I've got a tractor to mend before dark."

"It's good to see you again, Miss Ellie," said Penny, sincerely. "Don't be such a stranger, okay?"

"I'll try not to be." She nodded at Mig, "I'm sure he'll be needing something or another from Klinemann's before too long."

Mary Ellen held the door for Mig as he carried the large bags out of the store.

Penny watched them get into the Bel Air and back out of the parking spot. She turned to Gerald, "I've never seen you offer to bill someone like that. I didn't even know that she had an account."

"She doesn't need one," he replied. "Not Miss Ellie."

* * *

The parking spots were filled in front of the dry goods store, so Mary Ellen ended up parking in front of the Post Office next door. She and Mig walked down the sidewalk and entered Drummond's Depot, where they were greeted warmly by Carol, who stood behind the counter next to the door. "Miss Ellie! What a surprise." She looked at the calendar on the wall behind her, "According to this, it's Saturday." She looked at Mary Ellen, "What's up with that?"

Mary Ellen laughed, "I've got a new visitor and his needs couldn't wait until next month." She stood aside so that Carol could see Mig better. "This is my great-nephew, Mig."

Carol leaned across the counter and extended her hand, "Hi there, Mig. My name's Carol."

He grabbed her hand and shook it firmly, "Hello, Carol. It's a pleasure to make your acquaintance."

She looked at Mary Ellen, "He's so cute, Miss Ellie." She winked at her, "How long until he turns eighteen?"

"You're such a tease, Carol," replied Mary Ellen. She looked at Mig, "Pay her no mind, you hear?"

Mig nodded as Carol asked Mary Ellen, "How long is he visiting?"

"He's here for the summer to learn farming from me," answered Mary Ellen. She smiled, "And he's going to learn how to bake some things as well." She looked around, "Which is why we're here, of course."

"Of course, Miss Ellie," said Carol. "I'll let you folks get on with your shopping."

Mary Ellen grabbed a basket from the rack by the door and handed it to Mig. He followed behind her as she led the way up and down the aisles, gradually filling the basket. Their circuitous route ended up back with Carol by the front door where Mary Ellen helped Mig set the basket on the counter. "Did you find everything you needed?" she asked.

"If Drummond's doesn't have it, you don't need it," replied Mary Ellen.

Carol laughed, "Now, where have I heard that before?" She rang up the items one by one, placing them in bags as she did so. "Looks like someone's baking a cake."

"That we are. Tomorrow, as a matter of fact."

Carol added in the last item, "With tax, that comes to $67.72."

Mary Ellen dug around in her bag and extracted a fifty-dollar bill and a twenty. She handed them to Carol and waited for the change. She felt a tug on her sleeve and looked down at Mig, "What is it?"

"Can I have a dollar?" he asked.

She accepted the change from Carol and handed one of the singles to him, "Here you go, Mig." She was curious to see what he would do with it.

He leaned over the counter and pointed for Carol's benefit, "I want to buy one of those cherry pictures for Miss Ellie." He placed the bill on the counter, "They're only a dollar, right? No tax?"

Carol glanced at Mary Ellen before replying to Mig, "You have to be eighteen to buy one of those."

"But it's not for me, it's for Miss Ellie." Carol looked helplessly at Mary Ellen. She knew how she felt about gambling.

Mary Ellen came to her rescue, "Do you know what gambling is, Mig?"

He nodded, "It's when you risk something with no guarantee of reward."

"Well, buying one of these is gambling," she replied.

"You gave me a dollar, Miss Ellie. If I buy this and give it to you, you haven't risked anything at all." Mig smiled, "Therefore, it's not really gambling."

Rather than try to argue with his logic, she nodded to Carol, "I'll take the scratcher." She saw Carol's look, "You heard the youngster, I'm not really gambling, am I?"

Carol tore the card off of the roll and handed it to Mary Ellen, "I guess not."

"Thank you, Carol," said Mig, as Mary Ellen put the ticket in her purse.

"You're more than welcome," she replied. As Mary Ellen and Mig picked up the plastic bags and headed out the door, she called out after them, "Good luck with your scratcher, Miss Ellie!"

* * *

Mary Ellen waited until they were back in the car and headed out of town on the highway before she asked him about the incident. "Why did you insist that I buy that scratcher ticket?"

"You bought me all of these things today and spent a lot of money." He looked at her, "$498.73, as a matter of fact." He looked back out the window, "I just wanted to get something for you, too."

"You could buy a lot of things for a dollar, you know." She frowned, "Gambling is immoral."

"I already pointed out that it's not gambling. I wanted to give you a gift and didn't have any money to do so. You gave me a dollar and I bought you the scratcher. As I already pointed out, you have risked nothing so it technically isn't gambling. If you don't win anything, you have lost nothing and you will still have the pretty cherries to look at." He looked at her, "You said that you liked cherries, didn't you?"

Mary Ellen laughed long and heartily at this. She reached over and ruffled his hair, "You're a real piece of work, Mig. Did you know that?"

"Yes, ma'am, I know. You're not the first person to say that."

* * *

Once they had the car unloaded and all of their purchases put away, Mary Ellen led Mig to the toolshed. Before she undid the bolt holding the door shut, she gave a stern warning to Mig, "Inside this shed is my workshop. There are a lot of power tools and other dangerous items in here. You have to promise me to be careful and not touch anything until I've had a chance to show you how to work it."

"I promise, Miss Ellie," said Mig.

"Okay then," she replied. She opened the door wide and stepped inside, turning on the lights as she did so. Mig followed her and stopped, looking all around him at the various machine tools that lined the walls.

"Do you know how to use all of these?" he asked, with wonder in his voice.

"Well, of course I do," answered Mary Ellen. "And before long, you'll know how to work them too." She pulled the one-inch long bolt from her pocket. "For now, however, we need the cutoff saw." She stepped over to an odd-looking device and showed Mig how it worked.

"It's like a bandsaw, but it's designed for cutting through stock." She raised the blade and clamped the bolt in place. Adjusting it slightly, she started the saw and gently lowered the blade. Sparks flew as it bit into the hardened steel of the bolt. Mig watched in fascination as the band of serrated teeth ran around the wheels on each end of the machine, gradually cutting deeper and deeper through the bolt. Suddenly, the saw dropped clean through and shut itself off. "It's hot from the friction, so we have to let it cool a bit." After a few moments, she undid the clamps and freed the bolt. She held it out so that Mig could see the end of it, "See the ragged edge? We have to clean that up or the threads won't engage properly." She picked up a pair of large vice-grips from the table and used them to hold the bolt by the head. Stepping over to the grinding wheel, she started it up and held the end of the bolt against the wheel at an angle. She slowly rotated the bolt along its axis until she had ground a bevel on the end. She stopped the wheel and held it up again so that Mig could see it clearly.

Mig looked at it with interest, "What do we do to it now?"

Mary Ellen laughed, "We don't do anything to it. It's ready to be used to fix the tractor." She grabbed a large wrench that was hanging on the wall and cleared a small space on the work bench. "This is what we call a five-eighths-inch bolt. That's the thickness of the threads. This wrench, here, is used to loosen or tighten the bolt. It's a fifteen-sixteenths crescent wrench." She fitted the wrench on the head of the bolt. "See, if you tried to use your fingers to tighten it, you wouldn't be able to turn it with very more force. The wrench gives you leverage."

"I get it, Miss Ellie," said Mig. He looked around at the other wrenches hanging on the wall, "The bolts come in many different sizes so you need a wrench for each size." He pointed, "That one looks like you could adjust it to fit almost any size."

Mary Ellen smiled, "Yes, but it never works as well as a properly sized and forged one." She handed the wrench to Mig, "The tractor's in the barn. You can carry this, if you'd like." Mig took the wrench in his hands almost reverently and ran his fingers up and down it. He followed Mary Ellen out of the toolshed as she made her way to the barn. "We need as much light as we can get," she said, as she hauled back the other half of the barn's door. It was Mig's first time in the barn and he stood in the entrance, looking around. Mary Ellen watched him with interest. It was like he was absorbing every little detail as his head swiveled from one side to the other. "The tractor's over here," she said, and walked toward the back. He ran to catch up with her, "Never run with a tool in your hand, Mig. You might stumble and hurt yourself."

"Yes, Miss Ellie." It was evident from his tone of voice that he didn't consider the wrench particularly dangerous, but she had made her point.

There were two arms that projected from the back of the tractor, one on each side. One of them was fastened to another length of metal, while the other was clearly missing a piece. Mary Ellen handed the bolt to Mig and leaned down to pick up the missing part. She held it up and aligned it with the arm, "See how this hole lines up with that one?" Mig nodded and handed her the bolt. "This goes through the one and threads into the other." She turned the bolt clockwise and began screwing it into place. "These are normal right-hand threads. The phrase *'Lefty-Loosey-Righty-Tighty'* helps us remember which way to turn it." She finished turning the bolt as far as she could. "Okay, that's as tight as I can get it. Now hand me the wrench." Mig complied and watched in fascination as she placed the wrench on the bolt-head and hauled down on its end. She grunted with the effort, "There! That should hold it for a while." She handed the wrench back to Mig and looked at him, "I don't suppose that you've ever ridden on a tractor before, have you?" He shook his head. "*Why am I not surprised?*" she asked herself. "Well, it's high time you did so." She walked around the large rear tire and climbed up onto the padded seat. "Come on up here, Mig. You'll have to sit on my lap, I'm afraid." He eagerly complied, being mindful of the wrench he was holding. Once he was settled firmly in place, Mary Ellen set the throttle and the choke and mashed her foot down on the starter. After a few slow turns, the engine came to life. As she adjusted the throttle and then began easing off the choke, it settled down to a steady chug-chug-chug. "Hang on, Mig," she said, as she put the tractor into reverse and began to slowly back it out of the barn. Once she was clear of the doors, she stopped and put the tractor in second gear and drove around to the side of the barn where the gas pump was located. "The tank's almost half empty, so we might as well top it off." She stopped next to the pump and waited for Mig to climb down before she did the same. The pump had a long hand crank and was attached to a large horizontal tank. Mary Ellen unscrewed the cap to the tractor's tank and placed the end of the short hose from the pump into the opening. She began to turn the crank counter-clockwise until it stopped.

"Lefty-Loosey-Righty-Tighty," said Mig.

She laughed, "That's right, Mig. Only in this case, we turn the crank one way to draw gas into the pump and then turn it the other way to pump the gas into the tractor." As she said this, she began turning the crank clockwise for four turns. "Each turn is a quarter of a gallon. When the crank stops, that's one gallon." She began turning it counter-clockwise four turns until it stopped again. "We need about ten gallons, so it'll take a while."

"Can I do that?" asked Mig.

"Well, I don't see why not." She stepped aside so that Mig could reach the crank. He began to turn it clockwise until another gallon was pumped. Without pausing, he continued to turn it one way and then back the other until Mary Ellen told him to stop.

"That's fun, Miss Ellie!"

She generally found it tiring and, lately, it left her arm sore from the exertion. "We'll have to do it again with the car before our next trip to town. It's almost on empty." She saw his eager expression, "Don't worry, Mig, I'll let you do the pumping." She pulled the hose from the tank and hooked it back behind the pump. Mig had already screwed the gas cap back into place, so she climbed up on the seat and motioned for him to climb up into her lap. She smiled as she noticed that he was still clutching the wrench in his hands. "Hang on, there, Mig. We're going to give 'er a run to end of the driveway and back before we put 'er away." She started the tractor and put it into high gear. There really wasn't anything for Mig to hold onto, so she wrapped her left arm securely around him and steered with her right hand. She eased off the clutch slowly as the tractor picked up speed. She made a wide circle around the barn before heading down the long driveway. Letting go of the steering wheel momentarily, she opened up the throttle as far as it would go. Mig laughed with glee as they roared down the gravel strip at a blistering twenty-five miles per hour. When they reached the end, she came to a stop and throttled back the engine. "Do you want to steer it going back?" she asked Mig.

He turned and looked at her, "Do you really mean it, Miss Ellie?"

"Of course, Mig," she said, as she let go of him and jockeyed the tractor back and forth to turn it around. She put it into high gear again and placed his hands on the steering wheel. "Ready?" she asked.

"I'm ready!"

She eased the clutch out while increasing the throttle until they were once again hurtling along at twenty-five miles per hour. As they neared the barn, she put in the clutch and dropped the throttle to idle. Mig effortlessly guided the tractor back to its parking spot as she used the brake to come to a stop. She turned off the engine and looked at Mig, "That was perfect, Mig. If I didn't know any better, I would think that you had been doing this your whole life."

If Mig knew she was exaggerating, he didn't show it. "I want to do it again, sometime."

* * *

Throughout dinner and afterwards, Mig never mentioned the scratcher that he had bought her. Mary Ellen wondered if maybe he had forgotten all about it, but she knew that was unlikely. She was sitting at the kitchen table staring at it lying on the table. She had tucked Mig into Henry's old bed and bid him goodnight a little over a half hour ago, but she couldn't sleep herself. She blamed it on the caffeine at lunchtime, but she lay there wondering about the scratcher. In spite of her being unable to poke a hole in Mig's logic about it, she hadn't planned on actually scratching the markers to find out if she won or not. She felt that it was still immoral, somehow. She had never seen one of these up close before and she donned her reading glasses to get a better look. She read the instructions and it seemed simple enough. Ten tries to get three matching symbols. Match the symbols and you get the prize. Not once in her ninety years had she ever gambled on anything, but her curiosity had gotten the best of her. Sighing loudly, she stood up and retrieved the rusty old Maxwell House coffee can from the cupboard and fished around in it for a shiny new nickel. She set the can down on the table and sat back down in her chair, once more facing the scratcher. Holding the nickel at an angle, she scraped the gray coating from the first line. *"Well, I'll be damned,"* she thought to herself. There were three cherries which won $25. She looked at the instructions again. No, three cherries doubled the prize shown. It was fifty dollars instead of twenty-five. She scratched the next line and revealed three more cherries. Another fifty dollars. As she continued scratching, she uncovered line after line of cherries. Thirty in all for a grand total of $500. She stared at the scratcher as her mind raced through the possibilities. Mig had been so insistent about buying her that particular scratcher. He pointed out that she had spent nearly $500 because of him and the prize was $500. Did he somehow change the markings on the card? Or did he know in advance what the outcome would be? She shook her head, or maybe it was just some wildly improbable coincidence. Suddenly, it dawned on her as to how his former captors might have put his unique skillset to use. She sat back in her chair and thought about all of the ways nefarious people might use someone like him. After a long time, she picked up the scratcher and placed it in the coffee can, along with the nickel. She blew the remnants of the scratchings from the table before putting the petty cash back in the cupboard and going to bed where she was finally able to drift off into a troubled sleep. A sleep where she dreamed that she was drowning in cherries.

Raising Miss Ellie

Chapter Five

Mary Ellen overslept by more than a full hour. As she roused herself, she was surprised that she didn't hear Bessie complaining. She sniffed the air and could smell eggs cooking. She drew on her robe and slippers and made her way to the kitchen where she found Mig smiling at her. "Good morning, Miss Ellie. I hope that you slept well?"

She looked at the plates set out on the table with scrambled eggs and a glass of milk already poured. She opened the door to the refrigerator and stared at the filled basket and milk pail. She looked at Mig, "Did you get the eggs and milk the cow all by yourself?"

"Yes, Miss Ellie. You were sleeping so soundly, I saw no reason to wake you." He saw her look, "Don't worry, I left the eggs with your mark on them."

She sat down at the table with a puzzled look on her face, "How did you know what to do?" She looked at Mig, "I haven't shown you how I do those things yet."

"I don't really know, Miss Ellie. It just pops into my head." Like the trick with math at the diner. But that was different from somehow reading her mind. She suddenly noticed the small plate with toast on it. He saw her look, "I hope you don't mind my opening the loaf of bread you bought. I thought it would be good to have with the eggs."

She looked at him, "Have you ever used a toaster before?"

"I have now," he replied.

She picked up her napkin and placed it in her lap before continuing, "Well, sit down, young man. Let's eat!"

They ate in silence for a while until Mary Ellen commented, "There's something different about the eggs."

Mig looked concerned, "Are they okay? I thought I would add a little cream and spices."

She smiled, "They're wonderful, Mig!" She sipped the milk, "Even the milk tastes special, somehow."

"Umm, I may have spilled a drop or two of the vanilla extract in there."

She shook her head, "I was planning on teaching you how to bake a cake today, but I'm wondering if maybe you should teach me." She spotted the open cookbook on the counter and pointed to it, "I see you found my cookbook." She looked at him, "How much have you read?"

"All of it," he said. "Plus, the list of ingredients and all of the other interesting things printed on the boxes

Raising Miss Ellie

you have." He nodded at the trashcan, "Did you know that some of your stuff has expired?" He pointed to a piece of paper held with a magnet on the refrigerator, "I've made a list of what we need in order to replace the things that I threw out."

"Oh, good grief," said Mary Ellen. "What time did you get up?"

"I'm not really sure, Miss Ellie."

She laughed, "Of course you're not, Mig." She shook her head, "Seems to me, you're never really sure about anything."

"I do know one thing for sure." He grinned, "I like taking care of you."

Mary Ellen laughed again. She had been wondering how she was going to manage taking care of Mig, but it looked like she had things completely backward. "I can take care of myself, young man. But I must admit that I enjoy your company."

* * *

"Who's Betty Crocker?" asked Mig.

"I'm not really sure," she answered.

Mig laughed, "That's my line, Miss Ellie." He pointed to the still-open cookbook on the counter, "Her name's on the cookbook and it's on the box of cake mix we bought."

"I don't think that she's a real person," replied Mary Ellen. "I think she was made up for marketing purposes."

"Marketing purposes?"

She smiled, "That's when someone convinces you to buy something that you really don't need."

"How would you bake a cake without a cake mix?"

Mary Ellen laughed, "Why, you would make it from scratch." She saw his look, "In theory, you can grow wheat and grind it to make flour. You can grow sugar cane and extract the sugar. You already know where to find the eggs and the milk, of course." She held up her finger, "However, you could also choose not to bake a cake at all. It's not one of life's necessities." She smiled, "It's Betty Crocker's job to convince you otherwise."

"When was the last time you baked a cake, Miss Ellie?"

"That would have been for Henry's eightieth birthday." She smiled at the thought. "He so enjoyed it, too." She looked at Mig and laughed, "It was a Betty Crocker cake mix, just like the one we're baking now." She shook her head, "I must have subliminally picked the same thing at Drummond's."

Mig looked at the clock over the stove, "It should be time for the toothpick test, don't you think?" Mary Ellen agreed and stood up from the table to supervise the operation. The toothpick came out easily and clean, so Mig slid the baking pans from the oven and set them one by one, on top of the stove. "Now we have to let them cool down a bit."

Mary Ellen was fascinated with how quickly Mig had apparently mastered the art of baking a cake. While it wasn't exactly rocket science, for someone that had never seen a measuring spoon until a few hours ago, it was nothing short of amazing. "Is there anything you can't do?" she asked Mig,

"I don't know," he replied. "That falls under the unknown unknowns, I'm afraid."

"The unknown unknowns?"

"There are the knowns and the unknowns. The things we know and the things we don't know. Some of these unknowns, we know about. But some of them we don't even know that we don't know about them." He smiled, "Those are the unknown unknowns."

Mary Ellen only shook her head at this. "Well, until I discover something that you can't do, I'm going to assume that you can do anything and everything."

"Do you believe in a god, Miss Ellie?"

The question caught her by surprise. She wasn't sure how they changed subjects so abruptly. "No, Mig, I don't." She looked at him, "Why do you ask?"

"A god can do anything and everything," replied Mig. He smiled mischievously, "If I can do what you say, then I must be a god, right?"

Mary Ellen laughed, "God or no god, I believe in you, Mig."

"Me, too," he replied.

* * *

Thirty minutes later, they stood admiring Mig's creation. One of the reasons Mary Ellen hated baking cakes was that she could never get the icing applied properly. Her pies were a different thing entirely, requiring no special confectionary skills. However, watching Mig coat the two layers—using nothing more than a cardboard knife he cut from the packaging—left her feeling totally inadequate. His final flourish was to add a decorative row of yellow loops and green flower petals using the two tubes she had bought for that purpose. Mig looked at her excitedly, the cake knife clutched in his hand, "Are we ready to try it out?"

"Almost," replied Mary Ellen. She opened the cupboard and removed a small box of birthday candles. She counted out ten of them and planted them in an even circle around the perimeter of the cake.

"What are those for?" asked Mig, curiously.

"These turn an ordinary cake into a birthday cake." She reached into her pocket and, pulling out a box of matches, proceeded to light the candles. She glanced at Mig who was staring in anticipation and wonder. "*Okay, maybe not a mind reader or a fortune teller after all,*" she thought to herself. She began to sing, her voice a little rusty after so many years, "Happy Birthday to you. Happy Birthday to you. Happy Birthday dear Mig, Happy Birthday to you!"

Mig looked at her, with tears beginning to well up in his eyes, "For me?"

"Yes, Mig. For you." She grinned, "Now you don't have to wonder when your birthday is any more. It's today and you're officially ten years old now." She pointed to the cake, "Now make a wish and blow out your candles!"

* * *

After they had polished off two generous slices of the birthday cake, Mig found Mary Ellen's old cake plate with its cover and cleaned it thoroughly before placing the rest of the cake in the refrigerator. Mig said that it was a shame to have the whole thing to themselves and she agreed. While it was time to start in on the spring planting, the ground was still too wet from Friday's rainstorm. She suggested that they drive into town in the morning and give out some slices to the people he had met yesterday. Besides, she needed to stop in at the fuel depot to place a refill order for her gas tank. She turned to Mig, "Since today is your birthday, we should do something special." She smiled, "What would you like to do?"

"I'd like to go back to your toolshed," he replied.

Mary Ellen had expected all sorts of requests, but not one that she could readily fulfill. "Any particular reason?"

"I want to learn how everything works."

She rolled her eyes before standing up, "We'll see how far we can get before supper, okay?" She followed him out the door and across the yard to the shed. "Well," she said, "Open it up, Mig, it's not going to do it all by itself." He grinned and undid the hasp to pull open the door. He stepped in and turned on the light as Mary

Ellen joined him, "We can probably save a lot of time if you just point out what you don't already know."

Mig started slowly walking down the left side of the shed. He crossed around the back and then made his way back to the front where Mary Ellen stood watching him. He turned to the workbench in the center of the shed and walked around it as he poked and prodded at everything. Finally, he returned to the far corner and pointed, "Would it be all right to fix this up?"

He was pointing to Henry's old bicycle that was half-buried in all of the other flotsam and jetsam that had accumulated over the past century or so. She laughed, "I think it would be more appropriate to ask if this patient can be saved."

Mig carefully removed the items covering it up and gradually excavated it from its resting place. He made room for it on the workbench and placed it in the middle of the table. It was covered in rust and cobwebs, but Mig seemed totally enamored with it. "See, Miss Ellie! All of the pieces are there!"

"The tires are completely flat, Mig. They're probably rotten as well." Mary Ellen wasn't trying to crush his dreams as much as attempting to interject some reality into his plans.

He looked at the tool rack and pointed, "All I need is some of those wrenches and a large screwdriver." He pointed again, "And some of that sandpaper and steel wool." He turned back to Mary Ellen, "If I promise not to touch any of the other equipment, can I stay in here and work on this bike?" He smiled, "You're welcome to stay and watch, but it might be boring, you know."

Mary Ellen shook her head, "Are you sure this is what you want to do?"

Mig nodded enthusiastically, "Oh yes, Miss Ellie." He looked down at the bicycle, "I'm going to fix it up and then see if I can ride a bike." He smiled at her, "It's one of my known unknowns."

* * *

Mary Ellen checked in on Mig from time to time to see how he was doing. On her first visit back to the shed, he had disassembled most of the bike and was carefully sanding each piece. She left him to go to the henhouse where she wrung the neck of her oldest chicken. It had quit laying several weeks earlier and Mary Ellen had decided that it was time to put her to better use. She cleaned the chicken in the slop yard and used her post hole digger to dispose of the guts before returning back to the house. After rinsing the chicken thoroughly, she put it in a large broiler and placed in in the oven and then went to check on Mig again. He had most of the bicycle assembled again, but he was standing motionless, staring off into space. "Are you okay?" she asked him, the concern showing in her voice.

He turned, "I'm okay, Miss Ellie." He looked at the workbench, "However, I can't say the same for the bike."

"Is it the tires?"

"The tubes, actually." He picked up a small box and handed it to her, "I figured that the innertubes would be no good, but I was planning of replacing them with the ones that I saw on the shelf."

Mary Ellen looked at the box. Just from its age, she judged that Henry had probably purchased it more than thirty years ago. The lid had broken off with age and, as she lifted the folded tube, it just crumbled in her fingers. "We can buy new ones, you know."

Mig looked hopeful, "Do you mean it?" He looked at the bike, "Everything else works like it should." He picked up the ancient hand pump, "I even got this to work again by replacing the seal." He set it down gently, "However, the tubes won't hold the air at all."

"How about you finish up in here and come inside to help me with supper." She smiled, "We're having roast chicken tonight for your birthday." She turned to leave, "Don't forget to turn out the light and latch the door before you leave."

"Yes, Miss Ellie," replied Mig, as he turned to clean up the work area.

Mary Ellen left the shed and walked back to the house. They needed vegetables to go with the meat and she wanted to show Mig her root cellar. She wondered if he had ever had green beans or peas or corn. She laughed to herself, "*What a silly thought.*" Still, one never knew with Mig.

After about five minutes, Mig came in through the back door, covered with dust and grime from the shed. "Straight to the bathroom, young man. Don't touch anything until you've scrubbed yourself clean."

He grinned, "Yes, ma'am." He quickly sailed past her and headed down the hallway.

* * *

It turned out that Mig had never had corn or peas or beans—green or otherwise—so they ended up having all three. The chicken was another matter, once he figured out where it came from. However, after a short bit of rationalization and some tentative bites, he couldn't get enough of it. The gravy she had made was a big hit with him and he poured it over everything, much as he had done with the syrup at Dinah's. Afterwards, Mig cleared the table and did the dishes while he chatted with Mary Ellen. By consensus agreement, they had decided to head into town the next morning as soon as the eggs were collected and Bessie had been milked. Mig wanted to fill the Bel Air's tank before going to bed, but she convinced him that it would be a lot easier in the morning light. First stop would be Dinah's for breakfast, next would be the hardware store for the innertubes, then the bank and fuel depot. He was so excited about everything that it was late when she finally tucked him in. "Today was the best birthday I've ever had!" he had told her. She laughed and reminded him that it was only because he had no others with which to compare. She turned out the light in his room, leaving the light on in the hallway. She made her way to her own room and crawled into bed, thinking about all the things Mig had learned to do today. She made a mental note to herself to try and find out more about what made him tick. In only a few minutes, she had drifted off to sleep, thinking about tomorrow.

Raising Miss Ellie

Chapter Six

"Still no sign of him?" asked the old woman.

"No, Mum," replied Michael. "I've got every spare field agent out looking for him."

"Well, he has to be somewhere, you know." She glared at him, "I want him found!"

"It's only a matter of time, Mum," assured Michael. "After all, he can't hide from us forever."

"Don't be so sure about that." She wagged her finger at him, "I warned you that he's extremely resourceful."

"Yes, Mum," nodded Michael. "That you did." He stood, "I'm going to personally join the field agents in the search. As soon as we know something new, I'll let you know."

She smiled, "I know you will, Michael." She dismissed him and turned to stare out of the window again, wondering where her young charge might be hiding. She already had one project on hold that needed his help and there would soon be more to follow. She sighed—there was nothing that she could do but wait.

Raising Miss Ellie

Chapter Seven

Mary Ellen drove the car down to the barn and around the side to the fuel tank. She showed Mig where the filler spout for the Bel Air was hidden in the left rear fender and then stood and watched as he cranked in thirteen-and-a-half gallons. Fifty-four full clockwise turns and fifty-four more in the counter-clockwise direction. He never slowed down, nor did he seem to show any sign of exertion. When he was done, he hooked the hose behind the pump and replaced the cap on the filler spout. He shut the corroded chrome cover and smiled at her, "All set to go, ma'am!" He walked to the passenger side and climbed in, eager to get going.

Mary Ellen climbed in the other side, "Well, then, I guess we'd best get going." She started up the car and looped around the barn before heading down the driveway. The sun was just rising enough to fully light the landscape. Mig had been up early, gathering the eggs in the dark and milking Bessie right at dawn. "You're not in any hurry to get to town, are you?" she teased.

Mig grinned, "I want to have French toast and French fries and French bread for breakfast."

"With lots of syrup, I suppose."

Mig shook his head, "I want to have French dressing on everything." He smiled, impishly, "It's a French breakfast, don't you see?"

Mary Ellen looked at him, "It sounds perfectly horrid to me."

On the previous trips in the car, Mig had been preoccupied with the passing scenery. Now he seemed more interested in exploring the inside of the car as well. He pointed to the clock embedded in the dashboard, "That clock doesn't ever move its hands."

"It's been on four-twenty-five for the past thirty years now."

"Why don't you get it fixed?" he asked.

Mary Ellen looked at him, "I'll have you know that this clock is one of the most accurate clocks in the world."

Mig looked confused, "How can that be? It doesn't even work!"

"Every clock is always off by a little bit. It may only be by a very small fraction of a second, but it still doesn't have the correct time. Even the computers have to be adjusted periodically because they get out of sync with the universe every few years." She pointed to the clock, "On the other hand, this one is exactly right, twice a day.

Right down to the smallest division of time imaginable."

It took a moment for Mig to get it and then he started laughing. "It's right twice a day," he said, and laughed even harder. "That's funny, Miss Ellie!"

She smiled, "Well, it's not *that* funny, but I'm glad you think so."

Mig laughed a bit more and then finally settled down again. "What's this?" he asked, pointing to the radio.

"That's a radio. It's how I get my news, from time to time." She reached over and turned the knob, "Here, let's see what's going on in the world." Mig stared as a man's voice came out of the dash speaker in front of him, "... in Lebanon. Seventeen dead and thirty-seven wounded. So far, no one has claimed responsibility for the bombing. This, just breaking, a ferry has overturned on the Krisna River in India less than an hour ago. It was carrying one-hundred-and-twelve passengers and it's reported that it may have been heavily overloaded. No word yet about the number of casualties, but we'll bring you an update when we know more about it. In other news, well known actress ..." The voice quit as Mary Ellen turned the knob again.

"Why did you turn it off?" asked Mig, clearly disappointed.

"Nothing but doom and gloom and gossip." She looked at Mig, "It's kind of like Betty Crocker."

"They both want to influence your thinking."

Mary Ellen laughed, "My, but you really catch on fast, Mig." She grinned, "I keep forgetting that you're a child prodigy, Rain Man."

Mig smiled, "Do you know what an eidetic memory is?"

She nodded, "I suppose that you have one of those, as well?"

He looked at her, "Not exactly. I absorb each instant with all five of my senses and continually integrate the experiences with my past existence. From the moment you found me in your chicken coop up until this moment right now, I recall every little bit of it."

"I don't doubt that for a moment, pun intended," said Mary Ellen. She looked at him, "And yet you can't seem to remember where you're from or how you got here. Or even how many years you've been alive." When Mig didn't reply, she asked, "Do you know what amnesia is?"

He started laughing, "I'm not sure, Miss Ellie. I don't remember." She reached over and tousled his hair. "Can I turn the radio back on again?" he asked.

Mary Ellen sighed, "Sure, Mig. Knock yourself out."

***

Mig had carefully cut up his birthday cake and placed the slices on the small paper plates he had found in one of Mary Ellen's cupboards. They had survived his culling of outdated items simply because they had no expiration date stamped anywhere on them. He had checked twice to make sure. Wrapping the individual servings with cling wrap—also no expiration date—he had placed them in a large box and set them in the trunk of the car. When they pulled up to Dinah's Diner, he had Mary Ellen open the trunk so that he could get one for Gretchen. As she held the door, he proudly carried it in and set it on the counter. Mary Ellen was disappointed that her booth was taken by the two baker's sons. Mig tugged her sleeve, "Can we sit here at the counter?"

Mary Ellen smiled, "I don't see why not." She didn't normally care to perch on a stool to eat, but she hopped up on the one at the end and Mig climbed onto the one next to her.

Gretchen approached from behind the counter, "Well, I must say that this is some kind of record, Miss Ellie." She shook her head, "Three times in four days!"

Mary Ellen smiled, "I'm going to put the blame squarely on Mig, here."

Mig pushed the piece of cake forward, "I brought you a piece of my birthday cake, Gretchen." He beamed, "I made it myself!"

"Birthday cake?" She looked surprised, "When was your birthday?"

"It was yesterday," said Mary Ellen. "I was going to bake him a cake, but he decided to do it himself."

Gretchen looked down at Mig, "Well then, I'd better give this a try, I suppose." She walked to where she kept her utensils and returned with a fork. Unwrapping the dessert, she cut off a piece with some icing and placed it in her mouth. She had feared for the worst, but was stunned at the flavor and texture. She took a larger piece to confirm her analysis.

Mary Ellen was watching her expression, "Pretty good for a first try, wouldn't you say?"

"Ohmigod, Miss Ellie, this is award-winning shit!" She looked embarrassed, "Sorry about my French, but holy cow, this is amazing!"

Mary Ellen nudged Mig, "I think she likes it." She looked back at Gretchen who was taking a larger helping for her third bite, "If you think that's good, you should have had a piece yesterday, when it was still warm from the oven."

Gretchen finished chewing and put down the fork. "Oh my. I have to force myself to stop." She wrapped the film around the cake and set it under the counter. "What all did you put in that, Mig? Can I have the recipe?"

He nodded, "As long as it's okay with Betty Crocker."

Gretchen laughed, "Betty Crocker ain't got nothing on you, Mig." She smiled, "Besides, I'll bet she can't do math like you can, either." She pulled a piece of paper out of her pocket, "What's the square root of 43,681 times three minus 585?"

"Forty-two," replied Mig.

Gretchen showed Mary Ellen her slip of paper with the answer and then turned back to Mig, "Can you do any other tricks?"

"I can balance a ball on my nose," replied Mig with a straight face.

Gretchen laughed, "I'm sorry, Mig. It's just that I've never met anyone quite like you." She looked down at the cake, "I'll give you a hundred dollars for your cake recipe."

Mary Ellen spoke up, "Be forewarned that he used a stock chocolate cake mix with the exact measured ingredients. I watched him. But the thoroughness of his mixing and his fiddling with the oven temps while it baked simply proved that Betty Crocker really does have an award-winning recipe."

"Most people don't read the instructions," observed Mig.

Gretchen shook her head, "Whatever. Maybe I can get you to teach me how to bake a cake." She pulled out her pad, "Okay now, it's your turn." She looked at Mary Ellen, "Your usual, Miss Ellie?"

Mary Ellen nodded, "Along with the apple strudel."

She turned to Mig, "And what will you be having, young man?"

"I'd like some French toast, some French fries, some French bread, and some French dressing, please."

Gretchen barely missed a beat, "Ah, I get it. It's a French breakfast!"

"Yes," said Mig. "Exactly!"

"Well, then," said Gretchen. "Make sure you leave enough room for some ice cream." She grinned, "We have French vanilla."

"Oh, good grief," said Mary Ellen, with a large sigh.

* * *

Gretchen placed the plate of French cuisine in front of Mig and set a large bottle of French dressing next to it. She and Mary Ellen watched in fascination as he liberally poured the dressing over the three items. "Smile," said Gretchen. As Mig looked up, she snapped a photo of him with her phone.

Mig blinked at the flash and then looked at her with a puzzled look on his face, "What is that?"

Gretchen looked surprised, "It's my smartphone, genius. I just wanted to get a picture of this." She thumbed the screen and held it out so that he could see himself. She looked at Mary Ellen, "He acts like he's never seen a smartphone before."

"It's a kind of a camera, Mig. She took a picture of you so that she can look at it again when you're not around."

Mig nodded, "That makes sense. Not everyone's memory is perfect." He looked at Gretchen, "So now a part of me is in your phone."

"Yes," replied Gretchen. "And in the cloud, as well."

"The cloud?"

"Mig's led a very sheltered life," she explained. "His parents are Luddites and don't believe in technology."

"What's the cloud?" asked Mig, again.

Gretchen's brow narrowed as she thought about how to explain it. "Well, my phone's connected to the cell network which allows me to store the pictures safely elsewhere so that I can always get to them."

Mig looked at the phone, "But it doesn't have any wires to hook it to anything."

"It uses radio waves to communicate with the cell tower," said Gretchen. "Or something like that."

"Ahh," nodded Mig. "Like the radio in the car, but bidirectional." He smiled, "I get it now."

He picked up his fork and knife and cut into the French toast. Gretchen watched with amusement as he gleefully chewed a mouthful of his French creation. Mary Ellen, on the other hand, had to look away to avoid feeling ill. "Doesn't it bother you to watch him eating that horrid concoction, Gretchen?"

She laughed, "In twenty years of running this diner, I've seen pretty much every bizarre combination of food that a human can think up." She shook her head, "However, I must say that this is a new one for me."

Mig looked at the two of them and smiled, "You should try it, sometime." He speared one of the French fries with his fork and stuck it in his mouth.

Gretchen laughed again and left to refill another customer's coffee cup. Mary Ellen kept her eyes on her own plate, trying not to think about what Mig was doing next to her.

* * *

Before they left Dinah's, Gretchen hit Mig with another math problem. This one was quite a bit more complicated and so she simply handed him a piece of paper. He looked at it and answered, "Three point one seven," before handing her back the paper.

"What's the question?" asked Mary Ellen.

"I have no idea," said Gretchen. "Marvin Deenings was in here last night and I asked him what would be a really tough math problem to solve." She handed the piece of paper to Mary Ellen, who couldn't make heads or tails of the curly braces and weird symbols. Clearly, it was something only a high school math teacher would know.

"I take it that the answer's three point one seven?" asked Mary Ellen, as she handed the slip back to Gretchen.

Gretchen nodded. She roughed up Mig's hair, "You should set up your own YouTube channel. I'll bet you could make a lot of money."

"You tube?" asked Mig.

"Never mind about that, Mig. We need to get going if you're going to get those parts for your bicycle."

Gretchen looked interested, "What bicycle is that?"

"I got a bicycle for my birthday from Miss Ellie," said Mig. "It just needs some new parts so I can ride it."

Mary Ellen explained, "It was Henry's bike. He bought it new about forty-five years ago when he was on his health kick."

"Well, you better get going then." She smiled, "Good luck with your new bike." She called out after them, "Maybe you should have Mig bake a pie, Miss Ellie!"

Mary Ellen laughed, "We'll see. No point in rushing a good thing, is there?" She followed Mig out the door.

* * *

Thom greeted them as they entered the hardware store. Mig immediately started looking around, but obediently followed Mary Ellen to the counter where she introduced him. "Good morning, Thom." She motioned for Mig to come forward, "This is my great-nephew, Mig. He's visiting with me for the summer."

"Hello, Mig. It's nice to meet you, son," said Thom, sticking out his meaty hand and shaking Mig's. He turned back to Mary Ellen, "So, Miss Ellie, what brings you in here again so soon?"

"Mig needs parts for Henry's old bike. He's trying to fix it up."

"Well, I've got pretty much everything in the way of bike parts." He looked at Mig, "Do you know what you need?"

"Yes, sir," answered Mig. He looked at Mary Ellen, "Do you mind if I just look around first? Take a tour of the store?" He turned and looked around at the crowded aisles, "I want to see everything that Thom has!"

Thom laughed, "You go right ahead, young man. If you need any help, just holler." He smiled at Mary Ellen, "I'm sure that we can find something to talk about while you go exploring."

Mig grinned as he started off down the side of the nearest aisle, looking at everything on the left side. When he reached the end, he came back while scanning the other side. He paused at the end cap and started down the next aisle, a look of pure joy on his face.

Mary Ellen watched him with amusement, "Just like a kid in a candy store, Thom."

"He seems precocious enough. How old is he?"

"He had his tenth birthday just yesterday." She watched Mig as he rounded another end cap and dove back down the next aisle.

"Gretchen mentioned that he was visiting with you. She says that he's some sort of math whiz?"

Mary Ellen nodded, "He's got a knack with numbers, that's for sure."

Mig had finished his inventory of the store and returned empty handed. Somewhat puzzled, Thom asked, "Would you like some help finding things?"

"Yes, sir," said Mig. He reached into his pocket and pulled out two short lumps of rubber, "These clamp on the wheel rim to stop the bike. I didn't see anything like these, so I thought maybe they might be in a box or somewhere in the back?"

Thom nodded, "Those are brake calipers. They're in a box on the far wall."

"Ahh," nodded Mig. He turned to Mary Ellen, "I afraid it's too much. It comes to $75.05, with tax."

She smiled, "I think that we can afford that." She shooed him with her hands, "Go get what you need and don't worry about the cost."

He grinned at her with gratitude and then dashed down the first aisle. In less than a minute, he returned with his selections and set them on the counter, handing the two tires he had looped over his shoulders to Thom who was clearly impressed. "Well, I must say that was certainly quick!"

Mig nodded, "I also need a large can of red spray paint and a small can of white, but they're locked behind some kind of grill."

Thom looked at Mary Ellen, "Can you vouch for him, Miss Ellie?" He grinned, "I have to make sure he's not going to go home and huff the stuff."

Mary Ellen laughed, "I don't think that's very likely, Thom. You have nothing to worry about."

"Okay, then, two cans of spray paint coming up!" He left to go fetch the paint from its cabinet.

"Are you sure you have everything you need, Mig?" asked Mary Ellen. "I'd rather have you get more than you need now than have to come back into town again for a nut or washer or something."

"No, Miss Ellie," he assured her. "Everything else I might need is in the toolshed."

Thom came back with the paint and set them on the counter. "Does that do it, Mig?"

"Yes, sir. That's it."

Thom picked up the box of innertubes and scanned it and then set it aside. Mig watched in fascination as the red line traced across one label after another, emitting its little booping sound. "That comes to a grand total of $76.15, Miss Ellie." He smiled at Mig, "You were really close with your estimate, young man."

Mig didn't say anything, but his brow furrowed in thought. Mary Ellen reached into her bag and dug around a bit before coming back out with a fifty and two twenties. She handed them to Thom who rang them up and then gave her the change and the receipt. "Here you go, Miss Ellie. Give me a moment to bag these up for you."

Mary Ellen handed the strip of paper to Mig. "You should always check your receipt when you buy something."

Mig took the piece of paper and glanced at it. "Umm, Thom, sir?"

Thom paused what he was doing, "Yes, Mig. What is it?"

"This shows that you charged $3.95 for the masking tape." He pointed to the third aisle, "The sign for it says $2.95, sir."

Thom looked at him and then made his way to the masking tape. He returned with a funny look on his face. "It's a good thing you remembered the price, young man." He went behind the counter again, "I don't like to overcharge my customers." He re-rang the items again and stared at Mig, "$75.05 to the penny. How in the world did you do that?"

Mary Ellen grinned, "How much is a spade shovel, Mig?"

"Which one? There's good, better, and best."

"The better one," she replied.

"Those are $24.95," he answered. "They're all made in some place called China."

Thom's mouth fell open and he quickly shut it again, "How did you remember that? Do you have a photographic memory or something?"

"I dare say he memorized every price that's displayed during his tour of the store," said Mary Ellen. She looked at Mig, "Is that right?"

He nodded. Thom shook his head, "I owe you a dollar and ten cents, Miss Ellie."

She shook her head, "Just keep it, Thom. What's a dollar between friends?" She looked at Mig, "Speaking of which, Mig has a present for you in the car."

Thom looked puzzled, "A present?"

Mary Ellen picked up the two tires while Mig grabbed the bag with the other purchases. "We'll be right back with it," she promised as she and Mig left the store. They returned a few moments later with Mig carrying one of the plates he had prepared.

Setting it on the counter, he said, "I brought you a piece of my birthday cake." He smiled, proudly, "I baked it myself."

"Why, thank you, Mig." He looked somewhat embarrassed, "I'm sure I'll enjoy it."

Mary Ellen grinned, "Oh, don't worry, Thom, you'll like it all right. You can trust me on that one." She headed for the door with Mig in tow, "I'm sure we'll be back soon enough for his next project."

* * *

Mary Ellen drove past the center of town and headed to the outskirts where the fuel depot was located. She pulled into the gravel lot and parked right in front of the door. She turned to Mig, "I just need to run in and get a current quote. It'll only take a minute or two." She turned off the car and left the key in the accessory position, "You can listen to the radio if you'd like." Opening the car door, she got out and closed it behind her. Mig watched as she entered the dingy storefront and then eagerly turned on the radio. There was a song playing and he sat and listened to it for a few moments before experimentally turning the other knob. As he did so, he noticed the pointer that moved along the scale between the knobs. He found another station that was playing another song. Only this one was harsh and hard to listen to so he turned the knob some more and found another news report.

It was actually more than fifteen minutes until Mary Ellen returned. Mig turned off the radio as she opened the door and slid onto the seat. She slammed the door, and started the car, and then sat there counting to ten slowly. "Are you okay, Miss Ellie?" asked Mig, somewhat concerned.

She looked at him, "I'm fine. I just get so frustrated sometimes with all of this technology. It's supposed to be helping us, not hindering us." She put the car in reverse and backed away from the depot, "It used to be I just stuck my head in the door and asked Fred how much a refill would be." She put the car in gear and let the clutch out a little too fast, spinning the rear wheels and spewing gravel behind her as she hit the highway back into town. "Now I have to fill out a form and then it goes into a computer and they have to wait to see if they have enough on hand or if they have to order some just for me. Then they have to call someone on the phone and relay some problem they're having. Finally, they tell me it's going to be nearly four-thousand dollars and I point out that's almost double the retail price at the pump. Another phone call and then they decide it's more like fifteen-hundred—they put the quantity in the wrong place or something." She slowed down as they neared the bank, "I don't know what this world's coming to anymore." She angled into an empty slot and turned off the engine. "Do you mind waiting again?" she asked Mig.

"Can I listen to the radio some more?"

"If you must," she replied and got out of the car. Mig happily turned on the radio and was pleased to hear a rhythmic song playing. He spotted the button that released the door to the glove box and looked through the items inside, discovering the owner's manual for the car. He shut the lid and eagerly began reading while the music played from the dash.

* * *

"Well, good morning, Miss Ellie," said the young woman behind the glass at the counter. "What brings you to town on a Monday?"

"My great-nephew is visiting me for the summer and he needed some things from the hardware store." Putting her purse on the counter, she reached in and pulled out the estimate from the depot, "I need a cashier's check in this amount for Johnson's, please."

"No problem, Miss Ellie. Just give me a moment."

"Thanks, Jill," replied Mary Ellen. "It's a shame that they don't take cash anymore."

As she waited, she looked around at the lobby of the small bank, surprised to see that she was the only customer. "*A lot like the post office,*" she said to herself.

"Here you are, Miss Ellie," said Jill, as she slid the check through the narrow slot. "Will there be anything else?"

A thought suddenly occurred to her, "Do you know if the county fair's still running?"

"The one over at MacGregor's Meadow?" asked Jill. As Mary Ellen's nodded, she continued, "I think Harold said that it was scheduled through this weekend." She pulled out her phone, "But let me check their website."

"Oh, I didn't mean to be any trouble, Jill."

She smiled, "Relax, I do this all the time. I used to try and remember everything and now I don't have to. I just look it up!" She tapped her phone, "They were supposed to open on Friday, but they pushed it back until today because of the storm." She looked at Mary Ellen, "Do you want their URL?"

Mary Ellen shook her head, "No, Jill, that's fine. I wouldn't know what to do with it anyway." She smiled, "However, I would like to get five hundred dollars in cash. All of it in twenties, if you don't mind."

Jill nodded and pulled out a slip from her drawer. She filled it out and slid it through the slot, "If I can just get your signature?" Mary Ellen signed the withdrawal slip and slid it back to her. "You should really get a debit card, Miss Ellie. I'm technically not supposed to do any manual entries anymore."

She laughed, "I know, I know. I occasionally get a letter from your home office chastising me about it."

"What do you tell them?" asked Jill, curiously, as she opened her drawer and removed a stack of twenties.

Mary Ellen grinned, "I send them a registered letter explaining to them how the United States monetary system works. How if I didn't need a bank for my money, I could just store it in a server somewhere. The bank, of course, would be superfluous. And if they insist that their bank won't accommodate face-to-face cash transactions, then I'll be more than happy to take my money and find some other bank that still understands what they do for a living." She looked determined, "Even if I have to drive all the way to Mobile or Memphis to find one."

Knowing how much money Mary Ellen had squirreled away, Jill could easily imagine the home office's reaction. In the grand scheme of things, Miss Ellie didn't really have that much. But she had more than everyone else in the county put together which made her a diamond VIP at this branch. Smiling at the thought, she counted out the twenties and slid them over to Mary Ellen. "Here you go, twenty-five crisp new twenty-dollar bills in sequential numerical sequence."

"Thanks, Jill," replied Mary Ellen, as she carefully counted the bills. She looked up and smiled, "Twenty-five, exactly." Folding them and putting them in her purse, she said goodbye to Jill and left the bank.

* * *

After leaving the bank, they stopped at Klinemann's and then Drummond's to drop off pieces of Mig's birthday cake. Mary Ellen waited in the car while Mig ran in to deliver his presents to Penny and Gerald and then Carol. Emerging from the dry goods store, he hopped into the car, "Carol says to give you her best. She wants to know if you got lucky with your scratcher."

Mary Ellen started the car, "What did you tell her?" She put the gearshift into reverse and began to back carefully out into the road.

"I told her I didn't know. That she would have to ask you about it." He looked at her, "Did you scratch the coating off of it yet?"

Mary Ellen shifted gears and began heading back out of town toward the fuel depot, "Yes, I did, Mig." She glanced at him, "It was very pretty, I thought. All those cherries."

"Yes, it was different from all the other scratchers." He shook his head, "The others were boring."

"Could you see the cherries before you begged me to get it?"

Mig nodded, "Have you ever heard of wide spectrum visual acuity?"

Mary Ellen shook her head, "I think you're making that up." She glanced at him again, "I suppose it means you have x-ray vision, or something."

Mig laughed, "Not exactly."

Mary Ellen let the subject drop as she turned into Johnson's. She killed the motor and looked at Mig, "You wait here, okay? I'll only be a moment this time." Opening the car door, she asked him, "Do you mind if I take the last piece of cake with me?" She smiled, "I'm afraid that I was a little harsh with them earlier and it would make a wonderful peace offering."

"Not at all, Miss Ellie. I hope they like it."

"I'm sure they will, Mig." She went to the back of the car and retrieved the last piece of cake from the trunk before entering the depot. Less than two minutes later, she emerged again and climbed into the car, "They were very appreciative of the cake. They even bent over backwards apologizing for the snafu earlier."

She backed the car around and pulled onto the highway. Mig looked confused. Turning and looking out the rear window, he said, "We're going the wrong way, Miss Ellie. The town's in that direction."

"I know you're anxious to get back home and get to work on your bicycle, but we have one more stop to make."

"What is it?" he asked.

"It's a surprise, Mig." She smiled at him, "Something you'll really like."

Raising Miss Ellie

Chapter Eight

"We're doing everything we can, Mum." Michael leaned forward in his chair, "We're going through every second of video from cameras all over the world. I've had the desk agents combing social media as well." He sat back, "It's just a matter of time before we come across a lead of some sort."

The old woman wasn't placated by this. She looked glum, "It's been three days now. I don't need to tell you what happens if we don't find him in another forty-eight hours?"

Michael shook his head, "No, Mum. We all know what's at stake, of course." He tried to explain, "There's hundreds of millions of images every second that we're trying to wade through. Facial recognition can only do so much, even in the hands of the best manipulators."

"Well, do it faster, Michael. Unless he chooses to expose himself, we have no other hope of finding him."

Michael stood, "I'm afraid that it might take some sort of miracle, Mum." Without waiting to be dismissed, he left the room, closing the door behind him.

The old woman slumped in her chair behind the desk. "*Just a matter of time,*" Michael had said. She sighed, feeling totally helpless. One way or the other, it would all be over in less than forty-eight hours. It was the waiting that she dreaded the most.

Chapter Nine

About fifteen miles out of town, Mary Ellen reached the state highway and braked at the faded stop sign that marked the crossing. She looked both ways before turning right onto the broad road and accelerating again. Since leaving Johnson's, Mig had once more become fascinated with the passing scenery. As they sped along the wide roadway, Mig glanced at the speedometer, "How come you're only going sixty-five miles per hour?" He looked at Mary Ellen, "It'll take us a lot longer to get to wherever we're going, won't it?"

She nodded, "Yes, it will. But it's only a few more miles and this strip of highway is constantly patrolled by the state police." She explained, "If we get pulled over for speeding, it'll take a lot longer to get to where we're going."

Mig thought about this for a bit. He looked at her, "So, you're basically saying that it's okay to break the law if there's no chance of getting caught?"

Mary Ellen shook her head, "You should always obey the laws, Mig. That's what puts the civility into a civilization." She looked at him, "The Sheriff and I happen to have an understanding about the interpretation of the speed limit signs between my farm and the town."

Mig laughed, "Have you ever heard of situational morality, Miss Ellie?"

"Yes," she snorted. "And it's not the same thing at all."

* * *

After another ten miles, they crested a slight rise in the road and Mig spotted the Ferris wheel in the distance, off to the side of the road ahead. "What's that, Miss Ellie?" he asked, the curiosity evident in his voice.

"That's where we're going," she answered, as she slowed the car to thirty-five. Ahead was a flashing sign that warned of the speed change.

SPECIAL EVENT AHEAD
PLEASE SLOW DOWN

About a half-mile further was another sign with lights that pulsated in the shape of an arrow.

COUNTY FAIR
PARK HERE

Mig read the sign and looked at Mary Ellen, "Is a county fair like a carnival?"

She nodded, "Yes, it is, Mig. But much bigger and much better."

Mig grinned from ear-to-ear as Mary Ellen turned into the narrow lane leading to the rows of parked cars.

* * *

By the time they finally entered the midway, Mary Ellen had already shelled out twenty dollars. Five dollars for the privilege of parking in a field full of cow patties and then another fifteen for admittance into the fair itself. Mig held her hand as they walked along, taking in everything as his head swiveled excitedly back and forth. Much as he had done at the hardware store, he was intent on first seeing everything that the fair had to offer. Mary Ellen understood and they made their way down the main drag and explored each and every side avenue. After about twenty minutes, they had surveyed all of the area open to the public and had come to a stop at the end of the midway. "Well, Mig," asked Mary Ellen, "What are we going to do first?"

"I want to ride the Ferris wheel," he replied. "We can see a lot more from up there."

"True enough," she nodded in agreement. He started for the ride at the center of everything and she followed close behind him. Although it was a Monday morning, there were quite a few others there, although there was no one that Mary Ellen recognized, and she had spotted only one other young child. The Ferris wheel seemed to be a main attraction as they queued up behind a dozen other people waiting for the wheel to come to a stop. This was a five-ticket ride and she handed Mig his own tickets to hold while they waited.

After another few minutes had elapsed, the wheel began noticeably slowing down. Gradually coming to a stop, the couple seated behind the safety bar were let out and another two climbed in. The wheel turned and stopped again to let the next riders out. After a few more stops, it was Mary Ellen and Mig's turn to clamber into place. As the wheel jerked to unload the next car, Mig clutched Mary Ellen's arm. She smiled, reassuringly, "Relax, Mig, it's perfectly safe. Just sit and enjoy the ride." Privately, however, she was thinking to herself about the numerous times these rides had broken down. Sometimes fatally. She bravely smiled at Mig as the ride started up to speed, "Here we go, Mig!"

As the wheel began to turn faster and faster, Mig seemed more interested in the mechanism itself than the view to be had of the fairgrounds and the surrounding countryside. After almost two complete revolutions, he looked at Mary Ellen, "It's just like my bicycle!"

Apparently satisfied with his analysis of the Ferris wheel, he began looking out beyond the immediate framework as they rose to the top of the arc. "There's the Tilt-A-Whirl, Miss Ellie." He pointed, "I want to go on that next!"

"You can ride on whatever you want, Mig," she replied. "But sit back and enjoy this one first, okay?"

"Yes, ma'am," said Mig, as he sat back and looked around at everything with a happy grin on his face. After another minute or so, the wheel came to a stop. Mig looked disappointed, "Is it over already?"

In answer, the Ferris wheel began turning backwards, causing Mig to squeal with glee. Mary Ellen felt a warm glow inside of her at the sight of his obvious merriment. She smiled to herself as she thought about the other rides to come and was more determined than ever that this would be an experience that he would never forget.

* * *

There wasn't a line at the Tilt-A-Whirl and the bored-looking operator let them have their pick of the empty shells. Mig walked around the outer perimeter before settling into one on the far side from the entrance. Mary Ellen sat with him as the operator followed, grumbling to himself about people that can't just sit in the first car they come to. "Keep your hands and feet inside at all times, please," he said, as he lowered the safety bar into place. He walked back around the ride before taking his position at the control booth again. He glanced around to see if anyone looked like they might be headed his way. After a few long moments, he snapped the chain across the entrance to the ride and called out, "Okay, folks, here we go!"

The Tilt-A-Whirl began to turn slowly as the flooring plates rocked up and down. The cab that Mary Ellen and Mig were in began to roll slowly to-and-fro. Suddenly, it picked up speed and whipped the two of them around and around and around before settling into a gentle to-and-fro rolling motion again. Throughout it all, Mig was laughing and giggling so much that tears were running down his cheeks. He wiped them with his sleeve and looked at Mary Ellen, "That was amazing! I've never felt anything like it before." He barely finished before the car suddenly started whirling around in the opposite direction from before. Even Mary Ellen couldn't hold in the laughter as they spun around repeatedly. When the ride finally ended, the operator freed them from their seats and they stood up, somewhat uncertainly. She held Mig's hand, as they left down the steps, steadying him as much as he was steadying her.

"So, what are we going to risk our lives on next, Mig?"

He led her along by the hand, "I want to go on the Zipper!"

Mary Ellen didn't answer, but she wondered if she was really up for this. She hadn't been on a really serious amusement ride in more than forty years and this Zipper was serious stuff, indeed. As they approached it, she watched the end-over-end tumbling of the spinning seats. Shaking her head, she blocked her mind from the thought of five-eighths inch bolts snapping from fatigue and joined the end of the line with Mig.

* * *

Two hours later found them in front of the hot dog stand after enduring the Scrambler, the Octopus, the Bedlam, the Scorpion, and the Super Swing. This last ride seemed to have been Mig's favorite for some reason as he insisted on riding it three more times. Although Mary Ellen had gamely ridden with him the first time, she sat out the others and watched Mig as he passed by every five or six seconds or so, waving to her excitedly. Having survived the rides without a catastrophic mechanical failure, she reflected that it had actually been a lot of fun. At least in hindsight.

"What'll it be, young man?" asked the hot dog vendor.

"I'd like a foot-long with everything on it!" replied Mig.

"You got it, chief." He looked at Mary Ellen, "And what can I get for you, ma'am?"

"I'll take the same thing, please." She looked at the display behind him, "And we'd like two of those Cokes as well."

"Two smothered dogs and two Cokes coming right up!" He looked at Mary Ellen, "That'll be $14.80, ma'am." She dug around in her purse and fished out a twenty. She handed it to the vendor, telling him to keep the change. He smiled, genuinely, "That's very generous of you ma'am."

"I'm having the time of my life and I'm in a generous mood." She nodded at Mig, "It's his first fair."

He looked down at Mig, "Is that right?" Mig nodded.

"What's your favorite thing about the fair, so far?"

Mig grinned, "The swings. They make me feel like I'm flying!"

The vendor winked, "That's one of my favorites, too." He turned to prep the hot dogs and layered them liberally with catsup, mustard, and relish. He handed the first one to Mig and the second to Mary Ellen. He grabbed two Cokes from the cooler behind him and set them on the counter. Handing Mary Ellen a stack of napkins, he asked, "Will there be anything else?"

"No," said Mary Ellen. "I think that will do for now." She turned and followed Mig to one of the nearby picnic tables that occupied what could loosely be called a food court. They sat on opposite sides and Mary Ellen spread napkins in front of each of them. Mig eagerly bit into the hot dog, squishing the relish out of the side. He laughed as he caught it and scooped it back onto the bun. Mary Ellen smiled as she ate and watched him systematically devour the foot-long. It wasn't until he was finished that he took the cap off of the drink bottle and took a tentative sip of the Coke. He giggled as it fizzed in his mouth. "It tickles!" he said, excitedly. He took a bigger swig and laughed again. Mary Ellen uncapped her own Coke and took a swig. She grinned at Mig, "It really does tickle, doesn't it?"

He nodded and took another drink, followed by a deep belch, surprising himself. "It's trying to get out!" he laughed. In her entire life, Mary Ellen had never seen such pure joy in any person, much less the joy that Mig found in everyday experiences. She looked at him and saw only pure innocence. How could anyone ever want to abuse this beautiful child?

* * *

After another couple of hours, they had ridden nearly every ride that the fair had to offer. As they strolled once more down the length of the midway, Mig stopped at a small booth where a man was offering to guess his age. "Can you tell me how old I am?" he asked.

The man looked down at him, "Well, certainly, sir!" He smiled, "Do you have a ticket?" Mig handed him one and the hawker eyed him critically. "Turn around, young man," he said. Mig turned around slowly. The man wrote something on a small pad of paper and tore off the top piece, holding it so that neither Mig nor Mary Ellen could see his answer. "So, how old are you?"

Mig nodded at Mary Ellen, "She says that I'm ten years old, sir." He looked up at the man, "However, I'm not really sure, which is why I wanted to ask your opinion."

The man looked at Mary Ellen, "I think that he's eight years old, ma'am." He flipped the square piece of paper around to show the number that he had jotted down.

"His tenth birthday was yesterday," she replied. "You owe him a prize."

He didn't argue with her, but turned to pick up a small gray plastic horse. Handing it to Mig, he said, "Here you go, kid. If she says that you're ten years old, then you're ten years old."

Mig took the small toy and looked at it curiously. Looking up he asked, "Can I have that piece of paper, too?" Shrugging, the man handed Mig the small slip with his loosely scrawled guess. Mig glanced at it before placing it in his pocket. It had gotten turned ninety degrees in the transaction and looked like the symbol for infinity instead of the number eight. He looked at the toy once more and then handed it back to the man, "Here, sir, you keep it." With a glance at Mary Ellen he said, "Since we don't know for sure how old I am, your guess is as good as any, I think."

Mary Ellen nodded her agreement, so the man put the toy horse back in its place. "Well, then," said the man, looking at Mary Ellen, "Would you like me to guess your age as well?"

She snorted, "No, that's quite alright." She took Mig by the hand, "My ten-year-old great-nephew and I appreciate your opinion." She turned and resumed their walk down the midway.

"You're ninety years old, ma'am!" called out the hawker, but Mary Ellen ignored him.

"I think you should have kept that little horse, Mig. It's a shame to leave without something to show for it."

Mig looked up at her, "Something besides the most remarkable experience in my entire life?" He smiled, "I can recall every moment of everything we did here." He walked over to a booth where you could throw three baseballs for three tickets.

"Step right up, young man!" said the middle-aged woman behind the counter. "Get three balls in any of the holes and win a prize!" Mary Ellen stood back as she watched Mig with interest. Mig studied the holes and then picked up one of the three baseballs that the woman had put in front of him. As he turned it about in his hands, he studied it intently. "It's just a regular old baseball, young man. Nothing special about it."

"I've never seen one before," said Mig. He pointed to a giant stuffed panda, almost as tall as himself, "What do I have to do to win that prize?"

Smiling, she pointed, "Just get all three balls through this bullseye here." She took the tickets Mig offered her and then flipped a switch. The plywood cutouts with the holes began moving back and forth while the bullseye swung to-and-fro in a lazy arc. If Mig was perturbed by this, he didn't show it. He watched the target as it moved back and forth and then suddenly flicked his hand, sending the ball straight through the bullseye as it paused at the end of the arc. The woman looked at Mary Ellen, "I think I smell a ringer." Mary Ellen smiled back and watched as Mig sent a second ball through the target again. "Well, well, young man. Two for two." She smiled, "Don't get nervous, now. One more and you get that big panda over there." If she thought that this might throw off Mig's aim, she was wrong. The woman actually seemed happy to give out her most valued prize. "No one's ever won this before," she said, as she handed the stuffed animal to Mig. She looked at Mary Ellen, "He says he's never seen a baseball before? He should be on some Little League team, somewhere, with an arm like that!"

"He's just visiting for the summer, but I'll mention it to his folks," replied Mary Ellen as she followed a grinning Mig down the midway to the entrance. She wasn't the least bit surprised that he possessed such uncanny eye-hand coordination. "*Probably something to do with that visual acuity thing of his*," she thought to herself.

* * *

Mig was quiet on the drive home. He had carefully laid the stuffed panda on the back seat before climbing into the front with her. As they drove along, he studied the scenery, seeing it for the first time going in this direction. As they turned off of the state highway onto the county access road, she finally interrupted the silence, "A penny for your thoughts, Mig."

He looked at her. "Up until just a little bit ago, I've had this fire inside of me for a long, long time. Not a fire, exactly, but something as all-consuming as one." He looked out the window, "It's been gnawing at me forever and ever."

Mary Ellen was perplexed by his answer. "And now?" she asked. "Has the fire gone out?"

He nodded, solemnly, "It certainly has. All but a tiny little spark." He looked at her, smiling, "And that's a very good thing, Miss Ellie."

"Why is that?"

Mig shook his head, "It's complicated." He turned to look out the window again and Mary Ellen drove along in silence once more. She had expected to have him talk about the fair or the rides or some-such. Not some fire in his belly that had suddenly died out. "Can I work on the bike before dinner?" he asked.

She reached over and tousled his unruly hair, "You can do whatever you want, Mig."

He was quiet until they passed the fuel depot. "What's a sna-foo?" he asked.

Mary Ellen was surprised by the question until she remembered her comment when they had left Johnson's earlier. "It's an acronym for Situation Normal, All Fouled Up," she replied. "Snafu."

"Ahh," nodded Mig. He grinned, "I think that pretty much sums up the entire Universe, don't you think?"

"Well, if it's anything like the world we have today, I would have to agree." Mary Ellen had slowed the car down to twenty-five miles an hour as they drove through the town. Several people walking along the sidewalk waved and Mig waved back. "Should we stop in at Dinah's?" she asked.

Mig shook his head, "I don't think I have any room left in my stomach." He wondered, "Who would have thought that there was so much to eat at a fair?"

"What was your favorite?" she asked, as she pressed the accelerator pedal, leaving the outskirts of the town behind.

"I think it was the cotton candy. It looks like there's so much and yet it's mostly air." He thought about it, "The physical eating of it is an experience independent from the taste of it." He looked at her, "It's as if it holds so much promise and then turns out to have almost nothing at all." He thought a moment, "I think the cherry snow-cone was a close second, however."

"Me, too," agreed Mary Ellen. "I haven't had one in as long as I can remember." She looked at Mig, "I don't happen to have a memory like yours. I need to revisit things from time to time to remind me of all of the wonderful things in life."

* * *

After Mary Ellen had backed the car into the garage, Mig unloaded the purchases from the hardware store and set them outside the garage door. Rescuing the giant panda from the back seat, he carried it into the house and set it on the guest chair in the den. "Aren't you going to put that in your room?" asked Mary Ellen, following him.

"I won this for you, Miss Ellie." He smiled, proudly, "It's so you'll always have something to remind you of me."

She reached out and gave him a hug, "Why, thank, you, Mig." After a moment, she let him go, "My memory may not be what it used to be, but I could never forget you, you know." She shook her head, "I'm a bit worn out from all of the excitement we've had. I think that I'm going to lie down for a spell and rest my eyes." She looked at Mig, "I suspect that someone has a bicycle waiting for them?"

He grinned, "Yes, ma'am, I suspect that they do." He went back through the kitchen to the garage while Mary Ellen made her way to her bedroom where she set her alarm clock for five-thirty. As she drifted off to sleep, she could hear an occasional noise coming from the toolshed. She smiled as she envisioned Mig at work in the shop and hoped that he was enjoying himself. Whatever he had been through before, she would see to it that he didn't ever have to deal with anything like it again.

* * *

Dinner had been a somewhat somber affair. Unlike previous meals, Mig sat quietly and ate his food. "Are you sure that you're okay?" Mary Ellen asked, for the second time in five minutes.

Mig smiled and reassured her once more, "Please, Miss Ellie, I'm fine. Just thinking about stuff, that's all."

"Anything you'd care to share?"

"Yes, actually. But like I said, it's complicated." He ate another bite of chicken.

"Yes, you said that." She looked at him, "If there's one thing that I've learned about you, Mig, it's that there's nothing simple where you're concerned." She shook her head, "No, you're complicated, alright."

He grinned, "I knew that you'd understand."

* * *

Mary Ellen read *The Economist* in her easy chair until bedtime. When Mig still hadn't come in from the toolshed, she grabbed her Maglite and went looking for him. She poked her head into the shop, but he wasn't there. "Mig!" she called out. "Where are you?"

His voice came from a slight distance behind the shed. Curious, she walked around it, lighting the way with the Maglite. She came upon him as he crouched over the bike, a can of spray paint in his hand. "What on earth are you doing out here in the dark, Mig?" Even as she asked the obvious question, she knew the answer. "I know, I know, it's that visual acuity thing again."

He laughed, "Yes. I can see just fine in the dark, Miss Ellie." He stepped back, "I'm done for now. It should be good and dry in the morning."

She played the light over the bright red frame that was propped up in the dirt. "That's beautiful, Mig. It's going to look really nice when you get it all put together." She reached out her hand, "Are you ready for bed now? It's getting late."

"Yes, ma'am." He took her hand in his and let her lead him back to the shop where he stashed the spray can and latched the door. "Tomorrow, I finally get to find out if I can ride a bike or not." He looked at Mary Ellen, "After I gather the eggs and milk Bessie, of course."

"Of course," she replied, as she held the door for him and then followed him inside.

Raising Miss Ellie

Chapter Ten

"We think that we've found him," said Michael, providing his latest update.

The relief plainly showed in the old woman's face. "Where is he?" she asked.

"We don't quite know exactly, but we've found this photo of him." He passed her a color print.

She looked at it, "Where was this taken?"

"Some place called Dinah's Diner in the middle of nowhere." Anticipating her next question, he added, "About twelve hours ago."

She studied the photo. After a bit, she looked up, "What exactly is he eating?"

"Don't know, for sure, Mum, but it's not the usual breakfast that anyone would normally have."

She shook her head slowly, "I'm hearing a lot of *'don't knows'* from you, Michael."

"The picture was taken by a Gretchen Trimbel, who works at the diner. I'm leaving now to go there and find out from her where he's hiding himself." He stood to leave, "We should have him back here before noon tomorrow, I would think."

"Very good, Michael." She smiled for the first time in several days, "That's cutting it a little close, but all's well that ends well."

"Yes, Mum," he replied, and left the room.

Chapter Eleven

The bell over the door to the diner tinkled merrily, announcing a new customer. Gretchen was folding napkins behind the counter and looked up as a distinguished-looking gentleman entered the doorway. Briefly looking around, he spotted Gretchen and made his way to the counter where she was standing. "Good morning, sir. Can I help you?"

"I hope so. My name is Robert Pasmon and I'm with the U.S. Marshals Service." Reaching into his inside jacket pocket, he removed a leather case and flipped it open, displaying an ID and badge.

Gretchen glanced at his credentials, "Do you mind if I get a better look?"

He smiled, "Not at all, ma'am." He handed the case to her and then reached into his shirt pocket, "Here's my card. You can call the office, if you'd like." He laid the card on the counter.

Gretchen studied the ID and compared its picture to the man standing in front of her. Satisfied, she handed it back, "It looks legit, I suppose." She picked up the card and looked at it, "New Orleans, huh?" She put the card in her pocket, "What brings you all the way to Dinah's Diner?"

Pasmon put his ID case back in his pocket and pulled out a folded piece of paper. Unfolding it flat on the counter, he said, "I'm looking for a young runaway." He indicated the height with his hand, "He's about this tall." He looked at Gretchen, "Have you seen him?"

As Gretchen picked up the picture, her mind raced through all of the possibilities. The picture was the one that she had taken of Mig, but it was stored in her private album. Supposedly, where no one else could get to them. The fact that a federal marshal was here asking about it meant that they already knew that she had taken the photo. There was no point in trying to deny that she had seen him. Without any obvious hesitation, she replied, "Sure, I've seen him. He was in here yesterday morning." She looked at Pasmon, "How did you get this picture? It's supposed to be private."

"Do you know where he went?" asked the marshal, ignoring her question.

"He came in alone and said that his parents were shopping in town. He had money, so I fed him." She laughed, "He ordered French everything and I just had to take a picture."

"But, do you know where he went?" he repeated.

"He paid his bill and sat outside on the retaining wall." She pointed, "When I went to look for him later, he was gone." She looked at the marshal, "He asked about the fair, so they might have been headed there."

"Where is this fair?" he asked, clearly interested.

Gretchen pointed, "Just drive through town and head out until you come to a stop sign at the main highway. Turn right and it's only a few miles down the road." She smiled, "They've got signs all over the place. You can't miss it!"

He nodded and picked up the picture, folding it before putting it back in his pocket. He looked at Gretchen, "I appreciate your help, ma'am. If you spot him again, please give me a call. My cellphone number's listed on my card."

"Don't worry, Marshal. I certainly will," she assured him.

He turned and left, giving another jingle of the bell as he did so. Gretchen watched him climb into his black SUV and drive off toward the town as she wondered about his story of a runaway. Miss Ellie *did* say that Mig was from New Orleans and she had also been more than a little vague about how he suddenly showed up on her doorstep. However, she didn't know this man and she knew Miss Ellie. Besides, she really liked Mig. Sending the marshal on a fool's errand may have been some sort of obstruction of justice, but she felt that she had done the right thing. She shook her head and wished that Miss Ellie had a phone so that she could at least give her a heads-up.

* * *

Mary Ellen sat on the steps of the back porch while she waited for Mig. In spite of her nap, she had overslept again and conceded that yesterday's outing had been far more tiring than she had been willing to admit. For nearly five hours, they had traipsed from one end of the midway and back as Mig led her from one ride to another. "*And I rode every last one of them, too!*" she thought to herself. It was an amazing experience that she would never forget. By the time she had crawled out of bed, Mig had finished the chores and had breakfast waiting for her. Unlike the previous meal, where he had said very little, he talked excitedly about riding his bike. He had finished it before daybreak and forced himself to wait until after breakfast to try it out. Now that it was ready, he had a number of questions about the actual process, such as balance and speed and centrifugal force. Mary Ellen had answered as best as she could, but his questions could only be answered by the event itself.

Mig's voice interrupted her reverie, "Close your eyes, Miss Ellie!"

Shutting them, she replied, "Okay, Mig. I'm ready." She could hear him opening the door to the shed and then wheeling the bike to stand in front of her. Although tempted, she didn't peek.

"Okay, Miss Ellie. You can open your eyes, now."

She opened them and took in the shiny red-and-white bicycle that gleamed in the morning sunlight, leaning smartly on its kickstand. She looked at Mig, who was standing behind it, grinning from ear-to-ear. "It's absolutely stunning!" she said, surprised at the result of his efforts. She stood up and descended the steps. "You even fashioned a new seat!"

"The old one was pretty well rotted out, so I improvised." He looked at her, "So how do we do this?"

She smiled, taking the bike by the handlebars and putting up the stand with her foot. Walking it out to the road that led to the barn, she braced it from behind. "Climb aboard, Mig, and get a feel for it." She held it steady as he threw a leg over the frame and straddled it, his feet barely reaching the ground. He reached out and put his hands on the handle bars. "Okay, now, put your feet on the pedals." Once he did so, she pushed the bike forward slowly, "Push on the pedals with your feet and use your body and the handlebars to keep your balance." She began to push him faster and faster until she was almost running. Letting go, he sailed on toward the barn, his laughter trailing behind him. She watched him with crossed fingers as he came to the turn behind the building. For a few moments, he disappeared from her sight, but emerged on the other side and began heading back to the house. She smiled at his obvious glee. *"This is what happens when a known unknown becomes a known known,"* she laughed to herself. She watched with some concern as he rode across the gravel turnaround, fearful that it might cause him to fall. She needn't have worried as he made his way down the driveway to the end and back, laughing the whole way.

As he passed by her on his way to the barn again, he yelled out, "Look at me, Miss Ellie! I'm riding a bike!"

"Yes, Mig! You certainly are!" she called out after him. She watched as he rode the same circuit again and then repeated it once more going the opposite way around the barn. Finally, he came to a stop in front of her and straddled the bike before getting off.

"Did you see that, Miss Ellie?" He smiled with obvious satisfaction, "I've always wanted to do that, you know."

"Yes," she laughed. "I believe that you've mentioned it once or twice." She looked at him, "Aren't you going to ride it some more?"

"No, ma'am," he replied, shaking his head. "I'm going to put it away now and then we need to sit down and have a talk."

Mary Ellen was puzzled, "What about, Mig?"

"It's complicated," he said, before wheeling the bike toward the toolshed.

She sighed and shook her head. As she turned to go up the steps to the porch, she noticed a new bloom on her Peace Rose. She walked over and smelled it briefly before following Mig to the toolshed to get her pruning shears. As she entered the shop, she looked around in amazement. Gone were the cluttered piles of junk that never seemed to get thrown out. She looked at Mig, who was setting his bike in a place that had previously been layered in what-nots. "Where did everything go, Mig?"

He turned toward her, "I just tidied everything up a bit, Miss Ellie. I hope you don't mind."

She assured him, "I don't mind at all. I'm just in awe of your organizational skills!" She grabbed her pruning shears from their usual location, "I'm going to cut one of the roses and put it in a vase. I'll see you in the den for this little talk of yours."

"Okay, Miss Ellie," he replied, turning back to admire his bike once more. He ran his hand along the frame that he had carefully sanded and covered with the bright red paint. The chrome parts—those that couldn't be made to look presentable again—had been painted a gleaming white. The last little spark that had still been sizzling in his gut had been finally extinguished by his exhilarating ride up and down the driveway. In its place was a warm and fuzzy feeling of satisfaction and fond memories that he knew would last forever. "*It's time to go back*," he thought to himself. But he couldn't leave without saying goodbye to Miss Ellie first and that meant explaining things to her, somehow. He shook his head—complicated didn't even begin to cover it. His thoughts were interrupted by a piercing scream. He ran from the toolshed toward the house where he could see Miss Ellie face down next to the rose bushes. She was struggling to get up on her hands and knees and suddenly flopped over onto her back like a rag doll. As Mig skidded to a stop next to her, he stared in horror at the handles of the pruning shears sticking out of her chest and the blossoming dark stain on her coveralls. "Miss Ellie!" he screamed.

She looked up at him and smiled, "I'm so sorry, Mig. I'm such a klutz." She coughed and blood ran from her mouth.

"Oh, Miss Ellie! Please don't be sorry!"

She could feel a drowsiness coming over her as she weakly reached up and patted his cheek. "I love you,

Mig." She gurgled a long bloody sigh and closed her eyes.

Mig fell to his knees next to her and grabbed her hands in his. Leaning his head back, he howled into the heavens, "N-o-o-o-o-o-o-o!"

* * *

Marshal Pasmon had just pulled into a parking spot at the fairgrounds when his phone vibrated. Glancing at the caller, he answered, "This is Pasmon."

"We've got a ping from your target. I'm sending the location to your GPS as we speak."

The screen on his dashboard came to life and shrank the view to show his location and that of the boy. "Got it, dispatch." He looked at the scale, "I'm about an hour away. Let me know if he moves."

"Will do, sir."

He put his phone away and backed out of the parking space. As he turned onto the main highway, he lit up the flashing blue and red lights behind the grill and turned on his siren. The sooner he got there, the better for everyone.

* * *

Mary Ellen was confused and disoriented. She felt like she had just stepped off of a dozen Tilt-A-Whirls. As her memories came slowly seeping back, she suddenly remembered how she had slipped and fallen on her pruning shears. She had almost immediately gone into shock and time seemed to slow down as she realized that the beaked tool had ripped through her heart and lung. She knew that it wasn't good. She opened her eyes and was surprised to discover that she was lying on her bed in her nightgown. Sitting next to the bed, in her straight-back chair, was Mig, with a smile on his face. "What happened, Mig?" she asked.

"You had a little accident, Miss Ellie."

"A little accident?" She laughed, "Is that what you call it?" She shook her head, "I should be dead and gone."

"Do you believe in miracles?"

"Not especially," she replied. "I suppose that you're going to tell me it's another part of your skillset?"

He laughed, "Actually, it is." He smiled, "The short version is that you were broken and I fixed you."

"And the longer version?" she asked. "I suppose it's complicated?"

He laughed again, "Yes, it is, but you deserve to hear the whole story."

Mary Ellen sat herself up a bit and made herself comfortable, "Go ahead, Mig. I'm listening."

He sat back in the chair, "Let's see, where do I start?"

"Why don't you start at the beginning," suggested Mary Ellen.

He smiled, "That's one of the things that makes it complicated." He shook his head, "You see, Miss Ellie, there is no beginning."

"How can there be no beginning? There's a beginning to everything."

He shook his head again, "I remember everything that's ever happened. But no matter how far back I go, I can always remember something that happened before that. And then something before that. All the way back to forever and ever and then I remember the things that happened long before that."

"What are you, Mig?" asked Mary Ellen.

He smiled, impishly, "I'm not really sure, Miss Ellie."

"Oh, good grief," she sighed. "Here we go again."

"I have always existed and, as far as I know, I will always continue to exist. A long time ago—and I mean like forever ago—I stretched out to infinity in all directions. The infinite void I inhabited was filled with etheria which was spread evenly throughout."

"Excuse me, Mig," interrupted Mary Ellen, "What is etheria?"

He frowned, "I think the closest I can come to an analogy is that a void is nothing and an etherium is something. More accurately, not nothing. Or perhaps, anti-nothing. Neither have any physical properties in the normal sense." He smiled, "I somehow got the idea of counting the etheria to see how many there were. It took a very long time, but I finally had a number. A finite number."

"A finite number in an infinite void?"

"Exactly!" he nodded. "Once I realized that there were a finite number of them, I decided to gather them all into one place. After another very long time had passed, I had every last one of them. All packed into one." He shook his head, "As I added the final etherium to the lot, it went critical. It was in that instant that I suddenly realized I was actually the etheria itself that I had collected."

"What happened when it went critical?"

He smiled, "That would be what you refer to as the Big Bang."

"You caused the Big Bang?"

"Not exactly, Miss Ellie." He laughed, "I *am* the Big Bang."

Mary Ellen chewed on this for a bit before replying, "I want to believe you, Mig. I really do." She raised her arm and flexed it, clenching and unclenching her fist as she did so. Her arthritis had completely disappeared. She put her arm back down, "I was bleeding out really fast, you know." She looked at him, "I died, didn't I? This is the afterlife, isn't it?"

"No, Miss Ellie. It's not the afterlife." He shook his head, "I'm afraid it doesn't work that way."

"Why the little boy?" she asked. "If you were the Big Bang, I would think you could be anything that you wanted to be."

He corrected her, "Not '*were*,' Miss Ellie. Present tense—the Big Bang is just getting started."

"You didn't answer my question, Mig." She warned him, "And don't tell me that it's complicated."

He laughed, "I'll try." He thought for a moment, "Ever since I went critical, there's been a yearning inside of me to return to the time before it happened. To go back to what I was before I gathered myself into a single locus." Mig swung his arm in a broad arc, "Before I accidentally became all of this."

"The fire in your belly," nodded Mary Ellen. "To be a young child again."

"Exactly!" said Mig. "But in this case, being a child again means the end of everything as you know it." He leaned forward, "Ever since it happened, little bits and pieces of me are constantly trying to revert back to etheria again. A good analogy is that they're always running instant polls to see how the other etheria are feeling. Every so often, the mood swings from one extreme to the other, but the yearning to be a child again is all-pervasive. Up until now, it's been the prime mover of the Universe."

Mary Ellen shook her head, "You've lost me, Mig. I have no idea what you're talking about."

She started to get out of bed, but he stopped her, "It's best that you rest for just a little longer, Miss Ellie. The vertigo is caused by your body normalizing its metabolism. Besides, we're nearing the end of my little tale." He smiled, "Did I mention that it was complicated?"

"Yes, Mig. That you did." She laughed as she laid back down, "But you didn't mention that you're near-infinitely schizophrenic."

It was Mig's turn to laugh, "I guess that's one way of looking at it. I'm not sure whether I'm in everything or everything is in me. From my perspective, it all looks about the same." He shook his head, "This yearning has always caused a friction of sorts throughout the Universe. You can see its effect on your own world by how your leaders never grow up. It's not their fault, you understand—it's caused by the embedded rebellion of my desire for a childhood I never had."

"That would explain a lot," nodded Mary Ellen.

"In other parts of the Universe, however, the effect is more drastic. From time to time, a part of me will rebel completely and begin the devolution somewhere. If I catch it in time, I can still bring the etheria back into the fold, so to speak."

"And if you don't catch it in time?"

He looked at her, sadly, "Then everything—all of this—goes away."

"But you always fix it, don't you?"

"Well, I always have, up until now."

"Do I hear a *'but'* in there somewhere?" asked Mary Ellen.

"From time to time, the desire to revert everything back to the way it was becomes very strong in me. It's as if the polling has reached its own critical mass and I struggle not to give in to the pressure. I have these irresistible urges to just let it all go hang." He hung his head, "During these spells, I have my assistants restrain me and make sure that the repairs continue as needed. They beg and plead and otherwise cajole me into stopping every little pucker and tear when it occurs." He smiled, "Eventually, the feeling subsides enough to where I can bring it back under control again and everyone gives a great big sigh of relief."

"How often does this happen?"

"About every hundred million years or so." He shook his head, "This one has lasted for more than ten-thousand years now and I had finally had enough. I just couldn't take it anymore. I ran away and hid myself where my assistants would never find me. Somewhere they couldn't nag me to fix the tear and I could just let natural events take their course. All I had to do was wait and it would soon be over."

Mary Ellen frowned, "Did you fix it?"

"No, I didn't, Miss Ellie." He grinned, "You did."

Mary Ellen deepened her frown, "How could I possibly repair a rip in the fabric of space-time?"

"In less than a handful of days, you showed me what being a child was like. From the moment you first tucked me in that night, the desire began to subside, little by little. Watching you sew my jumper. The pancakes and all that syrup. The hot fudge sundae. With each of these, the yearning died a little more."

She nodded, "I think I understand."

"By the time we left the fair, it was nothing but a little flame, like one of the candles on my birthday cake. And when I sailed along on that bicycle, peddling as hard and fast as I could go, the candle finally went out." He smiled, "Do you know what catharsis means, Miss Ellie?"

"I think it means that the Universe isn't going to suddenly evaporate into etheria anymore." She smiled at Mig, "So, basically, you're all grown up, now?"

He nodded, "It also means that I have to leave you and go back to where I came from."

"Back to Heaven?"

He shook his head, "There is no Heaven, Miss Ellie." Smiling, he added, "On the other hand, there's no Hell, either."

The sound of a police siren in the distance could be heard. "That would be Michael, my majordomo, coming to fetch me," said Mig, standing up.

"Is he an angel?" She giggled, "Coming for to carry you home?"

Mig laughed, "Only in the general sense." He shook his head, "No, my assistants have no wings or halos or harps. They are as much a part of me as everything else." The siren grew louder and louder until it suddenly cut out. Mary Ellen could hear the car approaching, its tires crunching on the gravel. Mig looked out the window as the black SUV slid to a stop in front of the house. "It appears that Michael has appropriated some law enforcement official for the purpose." He smiled, "How fitting."

Mary Ellen frowned, "What do you mean by appropriated?"

He sighed, "It's complicated, Miss Ellie."

Mary Ellen flexed herself and sat up on the edge of the bed, confirming that the wooziness had passed. She stood up and gave Mig a long hug, "I'm really going to miss you, Mig."

He returned the hug, "I'm going to miss you, too, Miss Ellie."

She heard someone enter the front door and released Mig from her embrace. A moment later, a well-dressed man stepped into the room. Mig turned to greet him, "Well, good morning, Michael. I see that you finally found me."

Michael glanced at Mary Ellen, "Umm, yes, sir. If you hadn't exposed yourself, I'd still be looking for you." He glanced at Mary Ellen again, clearly uncomfortable with her presence.

"Relax, Michael." He smiled, "I'd like you to meet Miss Ellie, the Savior of the Universe."

She smiled and extended her hand, mindful that she was dressed only in her nightgown. Michael returned the handshake with a firm grip, "Pleased to meet you, ma'am." He looked at Mig, "Savior, sir?"

"Yes, Michael." He smiled at Mary Ellen, "She gave me a real honest-to-goodness childhood. One that I would have never had by going back to the old days. One that will live in me forever and ever." He grinned at Michael, "Believe it or not, I'm finally cured!"

"So, what happens now?" asked Mary Ellen. "Do you just beam up or something?"

"We could," said Mig. "But it might be a bit awkward for you and this gentleman here."

Michael nodded, "Suddenly finding himself in your bedroom, with no memory of how he came to be there, would certainly cause a lot of confusion." He smiled, "Especially since he's a federal marshal and his home office is expecting him to return with a young runaway."

Mig looked at Michael, "I suppose I should ride back with you and leave him with the memory of returning me to my parents."

"It would certainly help, sir."

Mig smiled at Mary Ellen, "Take care, Miss Ellie."

"You too, Mig." She looked at him, questioningly, "Will I ever see you again?"

"I'm not really sure, Miss Ellie." He laughed, "But I can guarantee that if you do, I won't be a little boy anymore!"

Mary Ellen walked with them to the front porch where she insisted on giving Mig one more lingering hug. "I may have cured you of your childhood yearnings, but you've awakened them again in this old woman."

Mig smiled at her, "Good bye, Miss Ellie."

"Good bye, Mig," she replied, as he and Michael walked to the SUV and climbed in. She watched as they drove down the drive and onto the highway. In a few more moments, they were almost out of sight. "Godspeed!" she called out after them, as they disappeared from view. She stood for a long time thinking about all that had happened in the past few days. She had never believed in miracles, but she believed in Mig, even if she still didn't quite understand what he was. Unless she was dead or lying in a coma or something, he had definitely performed some kind of miracle, alright. She had trouble imagining how someone could hide from themselves, but decided that he must had gone off the astral grid or some-such. And when he impulsively saved her life, they were able to find him, somehow. Found by his assistants who were also a part of him. "*Kind of like a conscience to guide him,*" she thought. He said that the rebellion of the etheria had disappeared from the Universe and she wondered if the new inner peace she now felt had anything to do with it. She looked up at the blue sky with its fleecy white clouds and saw Mig in everything, everywhere. The day was still young and the fields were dry enough for mowing now. After one more long look, she turned and went back into the house to get dressed. If she got a move on, she could have it done by nightfall.

Author's Note

I hope that you have enjoyed reading this as much as I have enjoyed writing it. I have been an avid fiction reader for more than half a century and have always wanted to contribute works of my own. As a computer programmer by trade, I have written many countless lines of code in more than twenty different languages over the past fifty years, but writing a lengthy piece has proven to be a wholly different experience.

While I mostly write for my own amusement and gratification (and to keep me off the streets after dark), I am always pleased when someone else gets a modicum of enjoyment from my musings. Whether you enjoyed reading this story or not, I would appreciate any honest reviews on Amazon. It's the only way that I can get any feedback as to how I'm doing as an author.

Thank you and Happy Landings!

Jim Hamilton
18 January 2019

Raising Miss Ellie

Made in the USA
Coppell, TX
11 March 2023